TORRID SUMMER

TORRID SUMMER

MARTHA MILLER

SAPPHIRE BOOKS

SALINAS, CALIFORNIA

A.I., artificial intelligence, to generate text that may replicate the author's style or genre similar to this work. The author retains all rights to use this work for purposes of generative AI training and development of any language learning system.

To the extent that the image on the cover of this book depicts a person or persons, such a person is merely a model and is not intended to portray any character feature in this book.

This and other Sapphire Books titles can be found at
www.sapphirebooks.com

Acknowledgements

Thanks to Terrence Andrik, Andy Lee, and the First Friday Writers' Group.

Dedication

To Cara, for her love and encouragement throughout the years.

Chapter One

In midsummer, after the second murder and before we had sex, a hurricane edged its way up the Gulf Coast. In Illinois, tornadoes came and went quickly, leaving a helluva mess. In Florida, with hurricanes, we watched the big chart on TV that showed it coming toward us, sometimes for days. There was no panic, many nailed up plywood, and others left town as the squall approached.

Alone at night when the thunder and lightning started, I fought my way through the storm's outer band toward the boardwalk and then to Magnolia's. My mother, who'd been convinced the storm would miss us, was occupied with her boyfriend. She'd told me to stay in and I'd be fine; this behavior had been typical for as long as I could remember.

I was trying to find Lyric. The bar should have been closed for the night, but there were a few cars in the parking lot, and I felt sure he was there. I stood outside the front window watching a few queens sitting around a table beneath the bare overhead bulb: makeup smeared, sequined garments hung from the meet rack, heavy capes lay across empty chairs, entertainers with knees crossed, a strap of a six-inch heel dangling off a toe. Lyric, his arm around Coco and his front chair legs angled a little bit off the floor, watched her tap a cigarette from her pack and offer it to him. He dropped his arm and leaned forward to put his chair squarely on the floor. The cigarette between his lips, he found a lighter and fired it up.

Above me, a canvas awning flapped in the wind. A thin layer of sand shifted beneath my flip-flops, and even though I stood firmly on the wet boardwalk, the surface felt slippery. Wind and sand stung my ankles, as behind me, the ocean exploded against the sea wall. Water, like rain, but not rain, created fast-running tributaries down the front window.

I reached for the door handle and found it stuck, but a hard push got it open. Stepping inside, I stood alone, dripping wet and cold. A strong gust of wind blew in, dispersing the cigarette smoke above the lighted table. Lyric leisurely turned his head toward me.

Struggling against the wind, I pushed the door closed, then picked up some papers that had scattered from the free-papers rack. One of them had blown open and was soaked. Even with this wind, the place smelled of sour beer and freshly cooked onion rings. Lyric waved and signaled that I should come back. Cold air froze my bare legs and arms. I brushed wet hair off my forehead and walked toward the group. An empty chair was shoved in front of me, and one of the queens passed me a dry, if not completely clean, towel.

"You want some coffee?" asked a tall queen with a deep voice and an expensive wig, whom I'd come to know as Bobbie Bobbins.

With the towel around my shoulders, I shivered and nodded. A full steaming mug was in front of me as if it had been waiting. I put my fingers around it and warmed them.

Coco said, "You came in the gulf side, honey, that was dangerous. What's coming over the sea wall alone could wash you away."

It made sense now, but I was from Chicago, for Christ's sake. I sipped the bitter coffee, and my voice trembled as I said, "I didn't know."

One of the queens started the jukebox and danced back to the table. Her hair was black and combed up in giant curls that night. Her cheeks were as red as a Russian doll's, and she had the face of Janis Joplin tattooed on her shoulder. "Care to dance, sugar?"

"Thank you, not now."

Lyric put his hand on my shoulder. "Soon as you recover, we'll head home."

Turning toward him to say something, I'm not sure what, I noticed he had dark and glittery mascara on his brows. I hesitated, then said, "Aren't you pretty?" Not really a question.

"Look around you," Lyric said. "We've all got our eyes done. Had a contest earlier." The only contest at Magnolia's that I ever heard of was the Biggest Dick Contest. The judges got so distracted the winner was never declared.

I looked for glitter on the others but was sidetracked by the TV, which was turned up as loud as it would go. An exhausted-looking weatherman said the next band would hit us within an hour. He finished with, "Citizens have been ordered to evacuate or take shelter."

I asked, "You all going to put up plywood?"

Lyric said, "Tried to buy some last night. Stores are all out. A little late to be out there hammering up plywood anyway."

"You're leaving in this mess?" Coco asked.

Lyric stood. "We don't live far away." He took my arm and helped me stand. "Come on. We'll go out the back."

With some effort, we shoved the back door open and descended three tall steps. The wind was deafening. Following the last step, my flip-flops sank into a pool of water that seemed to have no bottom. Lyric held both my hands and pulled until I got my footing. I lost one rubber sandal but tried not to think about it.

The parking lot remained the only place we could see anywhere. The shops on the boardwalk shared a large generator for as long as the fuel lasted. I heard someone cry out behind us and turned to see Coco, while maneuvering her way to her car, had gone ass-over-teakettle to the ground.

Lyric called out, "You okay?"

From her sitting position, she pointed. "I'm that first car over there. I can make it."

I was glad she didn't need help. I didn't want to go back, and I didn't want Lyric to leave me to help her.

We moved on.

Away from the parking lot, I only looked back once. Beyond the dim generator lights were vast white breaking waves along the shore and the darkness of the churning sea. Wind gusted. I couldn't hear anything, not even the crashing waves. The street was flooded. More than once, I held on to Lyric to stay upright.

My mother's house stood dark against the lightning-streaked sky. It felt good to be close to home and to be with Lyric, who had been through hurricanes before. When we reached the back door and went into the kitchen, I stumbled against the breakfast table. Mom had left a flashlight and three thick pine-scented Christmas candles. I picked up the yellow flashlight and flicked it on. The beam was dim, but at least there was one.

Home, I felt calm for a moment. "You have something to light these candles?"

Lyric pulled out his lighter and laid it on the table. "We won't use these until it gets worse."

"It gets worse?"

He folded his arms around me. "What on earth were you doing down at Magnolia's?"

I opened my mouth to explain that I didn't want to call my mother, although she'd told me to if I needed her, but I didn't see the point of explaining.

Glitter had been almost blown off Lyrics' eyebrow, which seemed funny, and I smiled and said, "I was alone. My mom's gone with her boyfriend."

"Mrs. Boyle says it's Charlie."

"Charlie? Great." The man had come close to killing her a week before.

I backed away. My arms were covered with goose bumps. I began to shiver. Later, I wondered if it was fear of the storm or Charlie. Her bruises weren't gone yet.

Lyric said, "Why don't you take a candle and go get some dry clothes on?"

"What about you?" Lyric lived in a small bungalow next to us.

"By the time I run home and back, whatever clothes I got would be soaked again."

"You would come back?"

He placed his hand on the back of my head and pulled me toward him. I could hear his heart pound, his heavy breathing. I realized that I too was winded. Then in a raspy voice, he said, "I won't leave you alone. If something happened to you, I couldn't stand it."

Of all the things I remembered from that night, the "I won't leave you alone" never left me.

But right then, I told myself that I could not, would not fall in love with Lyric. I had noticed his fondness for me, but he was a trans male and I was a lesbian. I'd been told the two didn't mate and I accepted that as true. Besides, I loved a woman back home, even though things were complicated right then. He and I were friends. That was all it ever could be.

Chapter Two
(On the plane)

My name is Jeannie Baker. I was at the beginning of my eighteenth summer, and the last place I expected to be was on a plane, watching the landscape grow larger, seeing palm trees for the first time, and listening to the landing gear lock in place as we prepared to land in Florida.

I was visiting my mother, a short visit in my mind. I had an open invitation from her since she came to my father, her first husband's, memorial. I hated her then and told her so, but we'd started Skyping once in a while. I'd tell her about my grades and how basketball had gone. Lately, she'd been telling me about moving to a new home, a rental; a friend of a friend who got transferred to London wanted to keep the house, just in case, so he decided to lease it out. Mom happened to work for the first friend. And she leased the house with an option to buy if the guy didn't come home straight away. It was close to the ocean where Mom worked at one of those restaurants that faced the gulf and claimed at sunset to have the view of surfers, sailboats, yachts, and coral sky reflecting on the water. She'd moved within walking distance of her work. I was happy for her but had no intention of living with her. My life was a mess, and I just wanted to get away for a few weeks.

My mother and I weren't best friends; hell, we barely knew each other because she abandoned me when I was ten. I came home from school the day she left, and she and all signs of her were gone. Until that time, she'd been a poor mother at best. I'd been left alone when she had a new boyfriend. But that was all I knew until my father got out of jail. Sounds like a soap opera, doesn't it? Then she left both of us. My grief about that time in my life seemed to be gone. I had swallowed it down into nonexistence. But it sneaked up on me sometimes. My father was a good man. Grandma said my mother leaving was the first real break I got in life. I believed that now. Grandma was my second big break.

What happened was, my mother had, without warning, left me with my father—he was one day out of prison and a stranger to me. Older now, I could forgive her. These days, she swore she was sober and determined to stay that way. She mentioned amends and a chance to make up for leaving me. Did alcoholics change? I'd investigated, and the chances were slim, but some did. A book I read said they had to be honest. If I knew anything about my mother, it was that she told whoppers, and no matter how often she did it, even after all this time, I'd fall for them. They weren't scary—just unnecessary.

Anyway, I felt I could take care of myself should she leave this time. Plus, I could see myself living a block from the ocean this summer and walking and running in the sand.

I didn't know whether to tell Mom I was a lesbian. It hadn't come up, plus Grandma told me a long time ago to avoid making decisions too soon about who I loved and who I would love. I'd be with Mom for a few weeks, not enough time to fall in love with someone new, so I imagined I'd stay a lesbian.

After I'd made Grandma promise to take care of

my dog, Diablo, to make sure he had food and fresh water in the summer heat, it was settled. I was going. As the plane was boarding, she told me to stay away from freshwater lakes and canals in the evenings because that was when and where the alligators fed. During the time I was in Florida, rain fell every day, and the canals stayed full.

All I knew about Florida was what I'd seen on Grandma and Joyce's *Miami Vice* DVDs. I planned to stay for three or four weeks, and I'd have a distraction from Legs, my girlfriend and lover, who was leaving me. Plus, I'd get to know my mother since she'd gotten sober; what could that hurt? Our history had some rough spots, but I tried not to think about them. Legs always said there was lots of drama between my mom and me.

My whole life, thus far, sounded like a country western ballad, yet I'd never run from anything—mostly because of my mother's bad example. Still, here I was, at the beginning of summer, running away from my first and only girlfriend.

❧ ❧ ❧ ❧

From the beginning, I'd known that Legs was the love of my life. I couldn't imagine a day without her. I was sure we'd marry and produce a couple of kids somehow, raise them, and grow old together. Joyce, Grandma's wife, tried to talk to me, just us in the kitchen, and said marriages that started at my age didn't last.

"There's supposed to be some time to learn about yourself before signing up for life. People change in early adulthood," she'd said. "No one knows what they want from life before they're thirty."

Thirty seemed a long way away. I knew what I wanted, and that was Legs.

When I was fourteen, I remembered my father telling me that my body would be ready for grownup love long before my chronological age was. Maybe marriage was like that.

What happened was, Legs and I argued in the middle of the night.

My second-floor bedroom was too hot during the summer. Grandma and Joyce's new house had a screened-in porch, nicer than that at the old house, but it had room for the same studio couch my father slept on during the summers of his youth. The bed was old and Grandma fussed at me, but I wanted it in the new house. She gave in. For years, she'd thrown a tarp over the thing during the winters. The mattress thus survived, and sometimes I thought I could smell my father's boyhood sweat. That touched a place inside me. Maybe he was with me on those nights. I sure wish he had been with me that night when Legs came to visit.

Legs, a name she'd earned from our girls' high school basketball team—no other team had a decent center—once lived across the back alley and slept in a second-floor bedroom whose light I had often watched. She and her brother lived with their foster family. In the summer, we'd travel back and forth and text often. She was hot in her room under the eaves but insisted she kept the window open and turned on a box fan she'd bought with babysitting money. That night had been a hot one. She'd driven a few miles to the new screened-in porch and came in the back door like the old days, then called out, "We need to talk."

A long time later, I realized that she hadn't sent me a text or an email like some morons would. She'd come to me, face to face. She'd had the grace to talk to me, to look in my eyes, to see my pain.

To begin with, I believe a lot is out of a person's control, but I was going to try to control it anyway.

So I asked, "What?"

"I'm getting transferred. I just found out this evening that I'll be moving."

I thought I must have heard wrong. "What?"

She knelt before me and said, "I'm ready to age out of the foster system, and my counselor wants me to move so I can get more education and some work experience. There's a group home in Miami."

"Does that mean you're going to see someone else?" That sounded so immature, but I couldn't help it. Tears filled my eyes. She hadn't said anything about someone else. In all that followed, she never said that, but that was where my mind went, and I was scared. "Do you want to date other girls?" Before she could answer, I said, "What will we be? Friends with benefits?"

"Jeannie, I love you." What was it I saw in her eyes? I later thought fear. Before I could say some more crazy crap, she leaned close to my face. "Look at me. Listen to me. You're hearing things I haven't said."

"I hear you. But this scares me. It could mean the end of you and me. Can you see that?"

She turned her head away from me, then said, "This separation will be hard. But we have to try. Otherwise, we might as well say goodbye right now."

Was that a threat? She'd never said anything so harsh to me. Trying to ignore the "say goodbye right now," I sat up. "Maybe Grandma would help you stay here. We could pay her back."

She shook her head and sat on the edge of the studio couch, where the mattress sank under her weight. Her short blond hair was pasted to her neck with sweat because she'd worn a nice outfit, a sleeveless top and matching pants, an outfit that I liked, but it was too warm. So she'd tried to please me. She stretched her long legs out before her and crossed them at the ankle. She was so beautiful. I said the first angry or maybe pathetic words that came to my mind. "But you told me with a girl like me, you wouldn't ever want anyone else, any place else."

She shifted to face me. "I meant it. I still mean it. But it's this or live on the streets again."

"Is this something to do with Malu?" Malu was a girl she'd had a sexual arrangement with before me.

"Malu? I suppose we might make contact. I'll be contacting you, too. A lot more often."

"So I've dropped back to friends with benefits?" I repeated the question, shaking my finger at her. "I've given you everything." I said this, not even knowing what everything was. Why was I so angry? I didn't like the things that were coming out of my mouth, but I couldn't stop.

"I'm just trying to save both of us a whole world of hurt," she said. "Can't we figure this out together?"

I remembered her words when the summer was over, as all summers eventually were. I thought about the care she'd taken with me even when, right at that moment, I was treating her like shit.

"A world of hurt" sounded like something from a country western singer's toolbox. "How? How are you saving me pain? If you wanted to do that, you'd find a way to stay here with me."

We had both known she'd soon be graduating

out of the foster care program, and she might be sent to a rare group home, usually meant for girls in more serious trouble than being fostered, or get cut loose. I'd had this dream that we would get jobs at Taco Bell, quit school, and get married. Like the girl in Tracy Chapman's *Fast Car,* only we'd do better. Of course, that wasn't plausible, but neither of us had a reasonable plan. I thought there was nothing we could do. It was to be Miami. Butterflies fluttered in my gut. How could we continue our love at such a distance?

Then I remembered that my mother had extended an invitation to spend some time with her in Florida. She lived just south of the panhandle, far from Miami but closer than the suburbs of Chicago.

I suggested that I spend the summer at my mom's or in Miami.

"You can't get into this program. I barely got into it myself." She stood, pulled a lawn chair close to me, and sat. "One important part of this is they're letting me bring my little brother. There's a school for the autistic near the house. Since he's a foster child, his tuition will be paid."

The need for her brother's care had occurred to me, too. I sighed.

She leaned close to me and brushed her lips on mine. "We can figure this out."

Then without giving me a chance to respond, she stood and left, letting the creaky screen door end our conversation with a whack. I heard her car start and watched the moving headlights as she pulled away.

I sat up on the studio couch and listened to the sounds of the empty night. I cried, and after a while, I stopped. I had nothing that would change her mind. She'd made that clear. Here I'd given myself to her. I let her touch me in my most secret parts. And all she said was that she was so sorry.

⁂

I couldn't get back to sleep. The thought of not seeing Legs was hard to accept. I had to figure out a way to see her in Florida. I seriously thought my mother might be an answer, but I hardly knew her. She might treat me like the old days, but staying with her might give me a chance to take a bus to Miami. So that wasn't all bad.

When we talked later, Grandma, although sympathetic, was against it. Then, when she saw that I was set on going, she sat me down in the kitchen over ice cream, something we had for serious talks, and tried to reason with me.

"If it were meant to be, you and Legs will find another way to be together. I know you don't…can't believe me, but can you trust me?"

I loved Grandma more than anyone in my life, except Legs. I wanted to trust her but couldn't. "I have to go, Grandma."

She nodded, then staring over my shoulder, said, "When a child is left alone over and over, no food, strange men in and out, with a mother who is more of a child than the child herself is, it does something to her. Honey, a part of you was broken long before your father came home. I'm not saying your mother didn't do the best she could with what she had, but it wasn't enough. Then what happened when your father came home? She left both of you: lock, stock, and barrel. Your father's death five years later threw more fuel on the fire. You're not seeing this situation the way other girls might because you've been left alone before, and this feels like more of the same. But it's not the same."

"I don't understand." Although I was starting to. If I admitted her argument had merit, I'd have to do the impossible, which was do nothing, and let Legs go.

I knew she was serious because she was letting her ice cream melt. For that matter, so was mine. "If that's true, what should I do?"

"Do the best you can and work with Legs to figure out how to maintain your relationship. In another school year, even less, you'll be free to join her, or maybe she'll be free to come home. Honey, this is just a short time in a long life. At my age, it's easier to see, but you and Legs will get through it and grow stronger for it. For most people, happiness is a decision. It's a little harder for you with your history."

I couldn't stay home and do nothing. I had to try to be with Legs no matter what.

When Grandma saw I was set on it, she stopped arguing.

❧ ❧ ❧ ❧

The next afternoon, I called and talked with my mother. She suggested the summer semester at some city college, where they taught dual credit courses, so I could get some college credits while still in high school. There was no way I'd be there long enough for a summer class, but when I told Grandma, she seemed less opposed. So it was sort of a lie. But we Baker women tended to be longtime believers in the inexplicable.

But nothing got past my BFF Ruthie. The night before I left for Florida, she and I sat on her couch, feet on the coffee table, eating Oreo cookies and drinking milk straight from an almost empty half-gallon carton that we'd been sharing. She thought I shouldn't leave; there were too many big things happening in my life, and running into the enemy's lair sounded dangerous. She'd known me since kindergarten and knew my mother and her behavior more than any of my other friends, or family for that matter.

Her words seemed extreme. She was fighting tears. Several times during the weeks that followed, I'd remember that night and what she'd said.

"I won't be gone long." I stopped and thought about it, then said, "I don't think of my mother as the enemy anymore."

She pulled two cookies apart, licking the icing, and picking at chocolate crumbs between her teeth. "No offense, but it seems the last couple of years, your life has been one disaster after the next, one loss after the next: losing your father, losing the home you made together, the broken leg, losing your spot on the starting team. Could it be that you're leaving Legs before she can leave you?"

Ruthie was the only one I'd let talk to me about my father. Legs had never seen him. I'd told her a little about my mom, but for some reason the subject of my dad was still too raw. My attitude might change someday, but for now, that was how it was. I'd had my share of problems, but I'd never run from anyone or anything. Yet here I was at the beginning of summer, running away from my first girlfriend.

Ruthie twisted two cookies apart again and said, "It doesn't make sense." She scraped icing off one cookie and stacked it on the next, so she had a double-decker Oreo.

"I tell you who I will miss. You. Are you sure you can't come with me?"

She laughed. "I start a new job tomorrow. Next time, give me a little more notice."

I missed Ruthie all the time I was in Florida. I texted her several times that first day and then less so as time passed.

I regretted the foolish Florida plan by the time the plane left Illinois. I asked myself how much I could shorten the trip. Legs or no Legs, I wanted to go home. Although I rarely talked about that summer, the things that happened there would haunt me forever.

With the roar of the engines and a sleepless night behind me, I dozed off, coming awake wanting Legs, thinking I'd crawl all the way to perdition for a taste of her lips.

Chapter Three
(*In Florida*)

When I deplaned, my mother was waiting at the luggage carousel. That day, she had carrot-red hair and black fingernails. If I'd told her that the color on her nails was way out of style even for women her age, it probably wouldn't matter. What did older women like her care about fashion? She wore calf-length olive chinos and a tight pink camisole with lace. The top of her arms hung a bit and jiggled. It probably would have been less noticeable if she hadn't had barbed wire tattoos just above her elbows. On her feet were colorful pink Crocs. She was an embarrassment for a minute or two until I looked around and saw other women dressed like her. I thought when people got her age, they should dress like other old people, which I guess she'd done.

Mom waved and came toward me smiling. Then she was there with an arm around me.

She got my red suitcase and asked if I could walk all the way to the car. She probably was considering my broken leg from two years ago.

I said, "Of course." Luckily, she didn't believe me.

Outside, she pointed to a crowded bench. "Wait over there with your suitcase, and I'll bring the car around."

As I walked toward the crammed bench pulling

my luggage, I felt like I was walking through a wall of humidity. The weather got hot at home, but this seemed worse. An attractive young guy stood and gave me his seat. I tried to argue but was glad when he insisted.

Soon a shuttle bus pulled up, and the bench emptied. The guy sat next to me.

"Are you from Florida?" he asked.

"Visiting."

He nodded.

When my mother's car came, I stood and pulled my suitcase behind me.

The guy asked, "Do you need help?"

I turned and smiled. "No thanks."

Instead of giving it up, he helped Mom get my luggage into the trunk, and after I was seated, he stepped back and waved. "Have a nice visit."

"Thank you." To myself, I said, "I hope I can make it two weeks." I would try to last that long. What difference did it make where I licked my wounds? Maybe Legs would miss me. I hoped she'd realize who she was quitting. I imagined that I'd get to my mother's house and my phone would be ringing. It would be Legs pleading with me to come back, and together we'd figure something out. Then I'd give the knife a little twist and tell her no.

As Mom blended in with the traffic, I noticed that the roads were wet, yet the sun shone fiercely. "Has it rained?"

"Stormed. It storms almost every afternoon this time of year. You'll get used to it."

The car's air conditioner blasted. My mother turned her head and smiled. "He seemed nice."

I shrugged.

"You don't like good-looking boys? What? You

dating girls now?"

I was pretty sure she was fishing, but I said, "What do you think you know?"

"Well…someone told me…"

She dragged it out, so I said, "I don't care if it's on the front page of the *Chicago Tribune*. It's over now anyway."

"That so?"

My tone cut her off. "Can we talk about something else?"

It worked. Mom said, "Okay," and didn't utter another word all the way to her house.

Even in the car from the airport, I hoped to hear my phone ring. Pulling it from my pocket, I checked the bars and the battery. All was good. My anger and love felt all mixed up. A knot of anguish burned in my chest. I'd thought we'd be together forever. I'd imagined a future with just the two of us. If that sounded crazy to older people, so be it. I believed it.

Two years ago, when my leg had been broken, Legs came to the hospital every day, all sweet and gentle. I'd come home on crutches, and Grandma made a bedroom for me on the back porch so I didn't have to use the stairs until I was ready. Legs saw me a lot then. I'd taken it for granted because, at the time, she lived so near and because we were in love.

Tears stung my eyes. I tried to push the thoughts back.

❧❧❧❧

My mother's house was a block from the Gulf of Mexico, one of those nondescript ranches that looked like most of the others on the block—hers was pink stucco surrounded by small palm trees. I dragged my suitcase out of the car's trunk and followed her inside. The house was freezing and reeked of cigarettes. Mom escorted me to a hallway and told me my room was the second door on the right.

"Go ahead and make yourself at home. The guest room has an attached bathroom with a shower. When you feel human again, I'll show you around."

I made my way toward the second door on the right, dragging my rolling suitcase with me. It was awkward, but I decided to ask for as little help as possible. The room seemed a bit warmer than the rest of the place, and it smelled of dust, like the attic at Grandma's. The room had a twin bed, a chest of drawers with a small TV on top, and a Spartan desk and chair near the single window. The closet door stood partially open; inside hung several empty hangers. On the back of the bathroom door was a full-length mirror, where a thin and tired girl looked back at me. My T-shirt was wrinkled, my jeans hung on my hip bones, and my eyes were red with puffy circles beneath them. Damn. I lifted my hair off my neck. At home that morning, I'd decided my shoulder-length hair looked better down. Leaving my suitcase unopened in the middle of the room, I kicked off my sandals, lay on top of the covers, and closed my eyes.

When I woke, the room was dark. Someone knocked. My mother called out, "Jeannie?"

I said, "Come on in."

She flipped on the overhead light.

I blinked, then asked, "What time is it?"

"After nine. You missed dinner, but I thought you might need the sleep more." No longer in the pink camisole, she'd changed into an old Cubs T-shirt, hanging two sizes too big. She was braless.

My clothes and hair were damp from sweat.

Mom waved her hand in front of her face. "Why is it so hot in here?" She crossed the room and messed with the vent. "Oh, dear, I've accidentally left this closed."

"It's okay," I said, lifting my hair up again. "I'm all right."

She tossed a paper bag onto the bed next to me. "I got something for you."

Determined to say I liked it no matter what it was, I picked up the sack and took out a black T-shirt. "Thank you."

"Unfold it."

I held the shirt by its shoulders and shook it open. "Oh, my God." I was tempted to throw my arms around her. Instead, I said, "I love it!"

She smiled. Right then, she looked kind of beautiful. She was as happy as I was. "I thought you might like it."

I held the shirt up before me. It was a Slipknot tee with the Skeleton Bride on the front. I remembered the album but hadn't known it was on a T-shirt. "I didn't know they made these."

"A girl from work and I went to a swap meet down by Orlando just before Christmas. She told me a woman had a T-shirt tent, and she could find whatever you wanted. She had a bunch of Slipknot stuff. That one was on the bottom of a big stack. I thought you might like it because it's kind of pretty and scary with flames from the dress and a skull of the bride's face. Plus, Grandma Sylvia told me that when you got hurt the summer before last, they had to cut your only Slipknot shirt off. So I've been saving this one for you."

I must have thanked her ten times before I realized she'd told me she'd talked to Grandma. Keeping those two worlds apart seemed impossible.

She said, "I hope it fits."

I took a quick look at the collar. Small. Just right as long as it didn't shrink in the dryer. I said, "Exactly my size. Thank you again."

Mom asked, "You hungry? I could make a sandwich."

"Just thirsty."

"Come on in the kitchen," she said. "You like orange juice? This is Florida, and we're big on fruit juice."

I left the shirt spread out on the bed and followed her down the hall and into a huge bright kitchen with white cabinets and black countertops lightly covered with sparkles. All the appliances were matching stainless steel, and an island stacked with newspapers and stained with coffee had three stools, one of which was pulled out.

I said, "What a beautiful kitchen."

"Isn't it? If my boss's brother decides to stay in London and keep his job there, I'm pretty sure I can't afford the option to buy, but I'm taking it one day at a time. We learned that in Alcoholics Anonymous. One day at a time." She sighed and added, "Seems a waste to have such a beautiful kitchen when I don't cook that much."

I slid up on one of the stools at the island, and she put a large glass of orange juice in front of me. While I drank, she moved around the cabinets and showed me where the food was, much of it stuff I liked as a kid. Froot Loops, Count Chocula, Fig Bars, and Pop-Tarts. She told me to help myself to whatever she had, and if

I wanted something else, just tell her.

Not worried about food or drink in the middle of the kitchen tour, I asked, "Does Charlie live here with you?"

She stopped and put her hands on her hips. "You like to get down to business, don't you?"

"I just want to know who I might meet in the hallway some night."

She laughed. "Okay. Fair enough. He doesn't live here. He visits when he's in town. He drives a truck and is away for days at a time. He has his own place. I may be over there at times. So you won't have to deal with him in a dark hallway."

She crossed the room to the sliding glass doors, hit a switch, and the backyard lit up with colored lanterns. I went outside behind her; a noise, a cacophony of buzzing, humming, and hissing: frogs, insects, and the sounds of several other creatures beat against my eardrums. I backed up a step.

Mom said, "You get used to that racket."

Several feet from the house, beyond a patio with lounge chairs and several flower boxes, was a huge in-ground pool, with its lights on beneath the water.

"You bring a swimsuit?"

"No." I had not. Mine back home was worn out; it didn't fit right, anyway.

"We'll shop tomorrow night."

The air was hot and heavy. Bugs circled all the lights. Although the sun had been down for a couple of hours, the concrete on the patio felt warm on my bare feet. Something cracked like a rifle shot, and I jumped.

Mom said, "The neighbors. That door slams at least once a day."

"Why?"

She shrugged. "There's a guy who lives there, works in a bar in town and belongs to a motorcycle group. Last winter, his son, Lyric, came to live with him. I guess his mother had it with the kid. Father and son do not get along. They have arguments, and before anybody says something irreversible, one of them leaves, slamming the door."

"How do you know all this?" I'd never thought my mother was interested in anyone but herself.

"A nosy old lady across the street. She's lonely, so she watches everything that goes on in the neighborhood, then tells anyone who'll listen. She doesn't know you're visiting, but she'll figure it out soon, then go down her phone list. I hope I'm never that lonely."

After we looked around, Mom said, "Come on, let's go back in where it's cool and quiet."

I set the rest of my orange juice in the sink and said, "Good night."

Then Mom said, "I have a computer with Skype and Zoom, door next to yours."

"Grandma doesn't have a computer," I said, but I was already thinking of Ruthie.

"Too bad." Then, she added, "I have to open, so I work the early shift tomorrow. Be home around four. Help yourself to whatever you need."

I nodded and turned toward the hallway. The last I heard her say was, "Sleep well."

I promised myself I'd shower in the morning and stretched out on the bed with my clothes on. I woke an hour or so later, hearing the neighbor's door slam again, then rolled over and went back to sleep.

Chapter Four
(*Day after arrival in Florida*)

The next morning, I woke buried beneath a blanket and a comforter. The room was freezing. I picked up my phone to check the time—nine fifteen. No calls, texts, or voicemail. I felt the twinge. I hadn't said I wanted a call from Legs; in fact, I'd said the opposite. Of course, she could act on her own free will and call me.

I made myself get out of bed.

Washing my hands and face, I noticed I was still wearing the clothes I'd worn on the plane. I stripped them off, reached into the shower, and turned on the hot water. On the ledge were a new bar of soap and some fruity-smelling generic shampoo. Hot needles beat against my back, and I stood still in the water for a long time. At Grandma's, the hot water would have been long gone. Eventually, I washed my hair, got out, dried myself, and pulled on a pair of shorts and a T-shirt, *sans* bra. Unlike Mom, my lack of support was unnoticeable.

In the kitchen, the coffee was already made, and I poured myself a cup. Mom had set out sugar and powdered cream, but since I was ten years old, I'd taken it black. Next, I opened a box of cherry Pop-Tarts. As a little girl, I loved them, but because we were usually broke, I got generic cereal covered with sugar. I was hungry enough to make short work of two individual packages, four tarts in all. I didn't toast them. My guts were full. I felt a little nauseated.

Sitting at the counter working on my second cup of coffee and looking at a *National Enquirer*, I wondered how many days it would take before out of boredom, I started stealing my mother's cigarettes as I did as a kid. And my old addiction would keep me smoking, even though I made a promise to my dad that I'd quit. I heard a splash and was startled. Beyond the sliding glass doors, I saw a stranger swimming in the pool.

Whoever it was swam a couple of laps, then floated on his or her back. I ran to my room and found my flip-flops. I wasn't sure why, but I wasn't worried about my safety. Nobody was going to swim a couple of laps, get out of the pool, and murder me. The sliding door made very little noise as I went out. Still holding my coffee, I walked up to the edge of the water without being noticed and called out, "Who are you?"

With a splash, he drew his feet under him, stood, and shaded his eyes from the sun. "Who are you?" he called out.

"I'm Jeannie. The redhead who lives here is my mother."

He swam toward me and pushed himself up onto the edge of the pool. With a big smile, he said, "Lyric Hughes. From next door." He was slim, and his eyes were large, sapphire with dark lashes, the kind a girl would kill for. "I keep the pool clean, and Alberta lets me swim all I want. Never anyone here this time of day," he said. "Or ever, unless Alberta has a party."

I repeated, "I'm Alberta's daughter, Jeannie."

"Wow. I didn't know Alberta had any kids. You gonna live with her now?"

"I'm visiting." I couldn't remember the last time

I'd heard my mother called Alberta.

We sat awkwardly for a short time, then he asked, "Mind if I finish my laps?"

"Go ahead." I set my coffee down, pulled my flip-flops off, then squatted, and sat with my feet dangling in the water. As he went in headfirst, I saw his back and spotted a snake tattoo slithering out of his black T-shirt, up his neck, and into his buzz cut. Turning over at the end of the pool and coming toward me, he turned on his back and I noticed a spray of freckles spread wide across his nose and cheeks. I thought he wore a T-shirt because of the sun on his fair skin. Florida sun was different than back home in Illinois. It was brighter—hotter.

Compared to the morning air, the water was cool. Through the slats in the latticelike pergola, I could feel the sun baking down on my head. One hand shading my eyes, I watched Lyric swim up and down the pool. After six laps, he swam toward me, coming up the stairs this time.

He sat next to me on the edge of the pool, his feet dangling in the water, his breathing hard.

Finally, he said, "I'm trying to grow some muscles."

Beneath his wet, black T-shirt, his upper arms were thin and ropey—but tanned. I tried not to stare. "What good are they?"

"Muscles? Just something I want."

I nodded. I could understand wanting something for absolutely no reason at all. That was good enough for me.

Lyric said, "I guess you could call me the pool man. I skim and check the chemicals. Never much to cleaning: big bugs, leaves, and whatnot. Test chlorine levels. Then I swim."

It made sense. As good of a deal for Mom as it was for him.

We sat making small talk for a few minutes: weather, school, Daytona motorcycle races, which his dad went to every year. I decided I should get inside and out of the sun. I stood and heard a voice behind me.

"Who are you kids? This ain't your pool."

I swung around and found a plump old lady with beauty shop-colored lavender hair, wearing faded jeans, a Marlins T-shirt with the neck cut out, and flip-flops like mine several feet away. She held a small-caliber rifle aimed at me. I squealed, stepped back, and felt the edge of the pool beneath my heels. I considered falling backward: better wet than shot.

Hoping I could make sense to her, I said, "I'm Alberta's daughter from Illinois. I'm visiting."

The old gal sucked air through her teeth, then said, "Alberta don't have no kids. She told me so herself." I watched the barrel of her rifle swing in small circles. "Now get on out of here."

I was about to get on out of there when Lyric touched my arm. Under his breath, he said, "Stand still, this has happened before."

I stood still.

Lyric said, "Come on, Mrs. Boyle. You remember me. I'm Lyric. Alberta said it was okay for me to swim in her pool."

She hesitated, tilted her head, eyes squinting, and looked our way, saying at last, "Sorry, Lyric, the sun was in my eyes." She lowered the rifle's barrel.

Lyric said, "This is Alberta's daughter. She's visiting." Then he forgot my name.

I tried not to stutter as I said, "I'm Jeannie."

Mrs. Boyle studied me. "You don't look nothing like Alberta."

To my relief, a uniformed policeman came around the corner of the house. He cleared his throat so as not to startle the old woman. Gently, he took the rifle from her, then he passed right by her and came toward us. "What's going on here?"

My heart pounded. A rifle and a cop were too much for one morning.

Mrs. Boyle called out, "That boy is a neighbor. Don't know who she is."

The cop turned to Lyric and said, "Who's your girlfriend?"

"Not my girlfriend, yet. This is Alberta Baker's daughter. She's visiting."

The cop looked me up and down. "Don't look nothing like her."

"I have my driver's license in the house. Can I go in and get it?"

The cop seemed to consider this, then said, "You two go on and get out of the sun. Jeannie, you better put something on your nose. You look like Rudolph."

I covered my nose with my hand and hurried toward the house, then stopped. The concrete was blazing hot on the bottom of my feet. I skipped a bit as I realized that I'd stepped out of my flip-flops beside the pool. I decided that it would be farther to go back and get them than to go inside. I hopped on toward the house.

Inside, I stood at the open door and heard the cop say to Mrs. Boyle, "I thought I confiscated your rifle."

She seemed pleased with herself, saying, "Waited

for Social Security Day and got this little .22 for a hundred and fifty dollars."

"Just because you don't need a conceal and carry permit in Florida doesn't mean you have the right to draw your gun on people."

"What else is it for? I live alone. I need protection. I was standing my ground."

"That's fine to protect you in your house but not at the neighbor's pool. These two are practically children."

Mrs. Boyle drew herself up and said, "I'm the one who called you. They were getting out of the pool, and I didn't want them to get away."

"You go on home now. If I hear of you drawing a gun on anybody else, I'll throw you in the slammer myself."

They argued, and their voices gradually faded away as the cop walked her home.

I closed the door, then went to my room, stood in front of the mirror, and checked my reflection. My nose was a little red. I had limited experience with sunburn, but I knew it would get worse. The fresh air outside made me sleepy.

I went into the living room and lay on the couch. I didn't know why it bothered me. I wasn't even surprised; Mom had no reason to tell these people she had a daughter, yet I felt she'd abandoned me again. If I didn't put it out of my mind, I was going to have a miserable two weeks. I turned the TV on to an old Western and dozed off.

Thunder woke me. My face burned. Through the picture window, I could see only darkness. Then lightning streaked across the sky and rain poured down. I got up and went into the kitchen. Through the sliding doors, rain drops bounced through the roof of the pergola, then danced on the surface of the pool water.

I'd decided to go out and get my flip-flops. Surely, the rain had cooled the cement. I opened the slider and found my sandals waiting for me. How thoughtful.

Next, I started looking around the house for something to put on my face. I found everything but skin cream. The coffee table had a half-empty coffee cup, a full ashtray, and four *People* magazines. I checked the hallway bathroom. The clutter was disturbing. The linen closet had some extra sheets and blankets. Only a couple of clean towels.

In the smallest bedroom, I found a chaotic office. Nothing as personal as face cream. At the end of the hall was Mom's room. I didn't want to go in there, but my face hurt. Turning the doorknob, I found it locked and immediately took offense. Did she think I was a thief? What the heck was in there that I'd want? Then the fact that Mom hadn't told anyone she had a daughter started aggravating me even more. She hadn't claimed me, and she thought I might rob her. I could have let it go until there was a gun held on me. She might have said something to at least one of them. Maybe she was ashamed of me and didn't want people to know she had a lesbian daughter. But it was she who asked me to come. Why would she do that if I was an embarrassment?

Back in the kitchen, I looked through phone numbers on the fridge and found her work number. The phone rang several times, and just as I thought I was going to end up leaving a message, Mom picked up, saying, "Alberta Baker. Sunset Dining."

"Hi. It's me."

"Jeannie?"

"Yeah. I got some sunburn earlier, and I can't find anything in the house to put on it. I'm getting little bubbles on my nose."

Mom seemed to sigh. But if she was disgusted with me, she recovered quickly. "Open the little cabinet above the dishwasher."

"Not much here."

"Is there a bottle of vinegar?"

"Yeah."

"Pour some into a coffee cup. Add a little water. If you can find a cotton ball, use it to spread the stuff on the burn. No cotton ball, dab it on with a tissue."

"It stinks. How will this help?"

"You're going to smell like a salad for a while, but it'll take the sting away. I'll stop on the way home and get some sun lotion and Nosecoat."

I stirred the concoction and took it to my room. Knowing I would never find cotton balls in all the clutter, I went straight to an empty box of tissue and settled on the toilet paper and dabbed some vinegar on all the sore spots and a few red places on my neck and upper arms that didn't hurt much yet.

After the storm, the sun blazed again, and I was happy enough to stay inside. I wondered what I was going to do in Florida for two weeks. I was homesick. Right then, I especially missed my dog, Diablo. When my father had died, I'd gone unwillingly to live with his mother, my Grandma Sylvia. The first and probably second thing she told me was not to feed that stray dog. I'd started feeding him routinely. He'd never let an old lady get the drop on me. If he were a mile away and I felt bad, he'd find me. He had done as much a while back when I'd fallen, broken a bone, and was lying in the rain and cold next to a flooded creek bank. He'd come right to me, sensed I was cold, and lay his warm back against me until Grandma and the paramedics found me.

People in Florida didn't leave dogs to roam, maybe because of alligators.

Later when Mom came home, she brought some sunscreen and Nosecoat. I'd never heard of Nosecoat. Probably no one in the Midwest had.

"Did you bring sunglasses?" she asked.

I shook my head.

"We'll get some after dinner."

That night, we ate pizza at the mall's food court. Afterward, we went to the Old Navy store, and I picked out a practical pair of sunglasses and the best-looking one-piece swimsuit I could find. I'd wanted a little two-piece, but Mom cleared her throat and shook her head no, even though right then she was wearing a low-cut T-shirt with a push-up bra. The navy blue swimsuit had little ruffles across the bustline that disguised the fact that I didn't have much up there. When I saw other girls my age, my thought was that the homemade sun-streaked colors in my hair were darker than the highlights the Florida girls put in their hair.

The sun had set by the time we got home. I dropped my filled-up shopping bags in my bedroom and went down the hall to the living room. I thought we might watch TV or talk or something. Waiting, I flipped through the TV stations. Several minutes later, I hadn't found anything I liked. Then I heard Mom's high heels on the hardwood floor.

I turned toward her and found her dressed like a bargain-basement woman. Her red hair was swept up, and she wore several pieces of jewelry. Her black dress fit like it was two sizes too small, with her boobs close to falling out of the top and the bottom barely covering her ass. If she bent down, everything would show. She also carried a beer bottle at her side. I tried to remember if she said we were going somewhere. Before I could say anything, she asked, "You'll be all right alone tonight, won't you?"

I nodded and remembered her telling me she was in AA. I didn't know what went on there, but I was pretty sure it wasn't drinking beer.

"Charlie is in town, back from a trip, and I thought I'd go over there for a while."

Relieved to hear he wasn't coming to this house, I said, "I'll be fine."

"Good girl." She looked at the beer bottle in her left hand and then at me. "Oh," she said. "This beer is for Charlie. Don't worry, I'll be fine." Then she waved her black fingernails and left.

At the door, I watched her car pull out of the driveway and her taillights disappear down the block toward town. I closed the door on the damp swampy heat and turned toward the messy living room. What could I do with this free time unless I watched TV all evening? I hadn't counted on being alone much while staying here. But remembering the first ten years of my life, I'd been home alone a good deal of it. I thought things would change. Didn't look like they had.

Back in Illinois these days, I had my friends, especially Ruthie, Grandma, and Joyce. I had a bookshelf with my favorite books. I had everything, including Legs. Or I used to have Legs. She would probably be gone before I got back home. At the other end of Mom's living room next to the large flat-screen TV was a bookcase. It was a mess, but I thought I might find something to read. On the top shelf, I found some pictures. Two of them were framed. One was of her and me. I was about four or five years old. We looked happy. Another was of her and a guy I didn't recognize. She was a lot younger then. I wondered how long she and Charlie had been together. She had a smile on her face in the picture with the man, his smile seemed strained. Maybe he was ready to leave.

What a terrible seesaw being in love was. It sends you flying up in the air, and next with your heart in danger, with the certainty that your desire will not be returned, you fall back down again. My guts churned when I thought about Legs. Things with us had been good for a long time, then they weren't. Mom and I were alike in some respects. Love made us give up things we needed and wanted. At the end with Legs, I could see myself surrendering to her will. It seemed that what she needed would always come first. I wondered if Mom had ever loved my father. He went to jail and left her. There were several other men over the years. We weren't in touch when she started up with Charlie. My estimation of him was well below sea level. I wasn't sure why. Maybe I blamed my mother's failures on him. I thought her self-destructive behavior could be to please him. For that, I hated him.

I found plenty of romance novels. Sorting through them, I found some Stephen Kings I hadn't read. Then I decided against a scary book while I was in a strange state, in a strange house, and alone.

I moseyed into the kitchen and surveyed the cupboards, opening them one by one. Not really hungry, I considered getting into my new swimsuit and going out to the pool. Nosing around, I looked under the sink. Cleaning products and not many of them.

Then the light in the room changed subtly. I turned. The security light out back had come on. I walked toward the sliders and found them locked. I'd read that in Florida, alligators found their way into private pools. My heartbeat picked up.

Someone stepped up to the door and tapped. The hairs on the back of my neck rose.

Chapter Five
(After Mom left for Charlie's)

The security light reflected on the sliding glass doors. Muggy heat penetrated the kitchen as I slid a door open. His hands in his pocket, Lyric waited for an invitation to come in. I swept my arm back.

He stepped inside and said, "Saw your mom leave."

"Her boyfriend."

"She'll be gone until after work tomorrow. Charlie has been out of town for ten days."

"How'd you know that?"

"Quickdraw, Mrs. Boyle from across the street. She knows everything."

My mouth dropped open. What kind of a neighborhood was this? "Did she run across the street and tell you?"

I wasn't reacting well to his visit. I missed my dog. My mind went over it again. Diablo would have let me know that Lyric was there before the security light came on.

Lyric smiled. "She has my cell number. She's fond of texting."

I ushered him to the kitchen island and pointed to the chairs. "You want me to make some coffee? Popcorn?"

"No thanks. Do you have any soda or juice?"

I went to the fridge, pulled out two cans of cola, set one in front of Lyric, and opened mine.

After an uncomfortable silence, Lyric said, "Does your nose-burn hurt?"

I said, "Only when I think about it. I must look like a damned clown."

"You should get something on it and cover it with gauze. A burn needs to heal from the inside first."

I tried to imagine my face with gauze on my nose. It was sad and funny at the same time. Maybe I'd cover it when I went to bed. "Mom had me put vinegar on it for the pain, then she came home with some other stuff to make it feel better. But I think the vinegar did as much as the stuff in a bottle. Anyway, it was too hard to wash off."

"Ah. That's what I smell."

"Back home, my grandma told me the old ways are best."

"Grandma? Alberta's mother?"

"My dad's mother." Then I asked, "Are you from Florida?"

He watched me for a moment as if deciding how to answer. I saw his face change when he'd made up his mind. He began, "My mom pretty much raised me. We lived all over the Keys. She was born and raised in West Texas but ran away when she was sixteen and met my father. They lived in New Orleans until I came along. Then they moved to Florida. Like my dad, she's a bartender. Unlike my dad, she never kept a job long. Dad has some old pictures of the two of them. She looks like a twelve-year-old rather than an eighteen-year-old with a baby. Anyway, they split up over another woman. Dad ditched her *and* the other one and came up here, leaving me with Mom. Then she and I had some big differences. She said I was an embarrassment and out of control. That's how I ended up here last winter."

He'd given me his life story in a few sentences. I thought for a minute and then asked, "Do you think you'll stay, with your dad I mean?"

He shrugged, finished his soda, crushed the can, and looked around. "Where's the…Oh, there it is." From where he sat, he tossed the can into a paper sack next to the fridge. It rattled against the other cans. Then he met my gaze. "I'll be nineteen on my next birthday and soon done with school. I'll have more options then. Dad and I don't get along. But I have some goals, and his help is necessary. I'm taking extra classes in the fall so I can graduate midterm. I want to go to college. What about you?"

Without thinking, I said, "I'm a senior in high school in the fall. I had college in my plans, too. Then my dad died, and I now live with my grandma. Not sure the money will be there when I'm ready. I planned on working this summer and saving money, then something happened, and I couldn't."

His brows wrinkled. "How old are you anyway?"

"Eighteen." I sometimes told strangers nineteen, but I felt honesty was important right then. I didn't think he was coming on to me. With guys, seduction was easy to spot, and I would have recognized it. Girls, not so much.

Lyric nodded. Then he looked at his watch and said, "I came over to see if you wanted to take a walk down to the beach."

"I guess. What's there?"

"Besides the ocean, there's a pier, a souvenir shop, a couple of bars, a tattoo parlor, and a hamburger joint. Farther down is the restaurant where your mother works. I like to go down there at night while the places are busy. I sit on a bench, watch people, and then mosey around. Seems things get interesting after ten."

"What about your dad? Does he mind?" I asked.

"Working tonight. He won't be home before three in the morning."

If Lyric had asked me to go throw rocks at a dumpster, I'd have done it. I needed to get out of the house, so I said, "Okay."

He stood and went toward the back sliding doors. "I'll change to warmer clothes and be back soon."

I decided to change into jeans and a T-shirt, then put some more goop on my nose, which made it look red and shiny. I sat on the couch and texted Ruthie. She didn't answer, so I kept my thumbs working on a long sad story about how depressed and lonely I felt. Even though she'd told me she went to AA, nothing had changed with my mom. I couldn't wait to come home. I missed her and my dog. I didn't send all my little complaints—just the biggest ones. There were two new voicemails. I hardly ever listened to the things, but I was passing the time. Both were Grandma. First just hoping I'd had a nice flight. And the second wished me a good night and asked me to call. I tried her right then, and she didn't answer. She didn't have voicemail or text or caller ID, and she thought she was old enough that she would die before she was forced to learn them. I shoved my phone into my pocket and waited.

⚜ ⚜ ⚜ ⚜

Lyric came to the back door at nine thirty. Ready and waiting, I grabbed the extra house key from a hook, and we left, walking.

"So you like Slipknot?" Lyric said.

I'd forgotten about my T-shirt and, for a minute, thought he might be clairvoyant. Then I remembered the Skeleton Bride and said, "Mom got the shirt for me. It's the one thing that gives me hope for the two of us. She went out of her way to please me."

"Maybe she does that more than you think."

"Maybe." I glanced at the sky, at a single sad star.

The night was cool and foggy. A boiling mist moved before us; we could barely see the sidewalk. The beach wasn't far, just a block and a half. I could smell it and hear it long before it came into view. A nervous voice inside me said the night sea was like a black hole and could suck me in at will. Not a strong swimmer, I would drown.

My mother couldn't see the gulf from her yard, even in the daylight, because several buildings blocked the view. As we got closer, I could hear music and voices. Lights penetrated the fog. The rear parking lots were jammed. The smells of cooking hamburgers and onions saturated the air. We walked in an alley between two buildings; sometimes the light was good, but there were dark places where Lyric held my hand until we were in the light again. A cool wind blew my hair around. The alley ended; we stepped high up onto a wooden sidewalk. It stretched both directions, connecting several different storefronts. Before us, I could see a lighted pier, and down past the pier were the bright lights of Mom's restaurant; the ocean was pitch-black out beyond the breaking waves.

Lyric took my hand and pulled me to the left. "This way."

We passed a tattoo parlor and a single-countered hamburger joint. The smells of hamburgers and fried onions masked the smell of the ocean. Ahead, music spilled out of an open door to a bar. A man and woman stood just beyond it, arguing. The guy was trying to calm her down. The woman started yelling, then she pulled back a fist and punched him in the arm. He gave her a little push, and her head hit the wall. Then he yelled, "Fine. I'm not the one who slept with someone else."

Abruptly, he turned and came toward us with hurried steps while still watching the woman. Lyric gently pushed me aside and put his hands up. "Whoa, buddy."

They collided. The guy apologized. "Sorry, man, I was distracted."

From where I stood, I could see he'd been drinking—a lot.

Lyric said, "No problem. You driving?"

"I'm on foot. Jezebel over there brought her car."

He stepped around Lyric and staggered on. As we went toward a bar named Magnolia's, the woman ran after her drunken boyfriend, husband, or whatever he was to her.

Several people stood around an open door, smoking, talking, and laughing. A guy just inside behind a cash register on a stool greeted Lyric like an old friend and then with a somewhat raspy voice asked, "How old is your girlfriend?"

"Nineteen," I cut in.

He shook his finger at us. "I don't want to see you with alcohol in your hands."

Lyric nodded and passed the guy a couple of dollars. I hadn't known we were going to be spending money. I'd put a twenty in my pocket, just in case, and left my purse at home. If the guy had asked for an ID,

I'd be screwed—not only because I wasn't nineteen, but Grandma had warned me that my Land of Lincoln driver's license wouldn't impress people down South, so I wasn't to flash it around.

Inside, a large room was lit by neon beer signs with a mirror behind the bar reflecting bottle colors that added to the dim light.

"What kind of place is this?" I asked.

"The best kind."

I followed Lyric to the bar, and a tall man in a wig and makeup greeted us. Lyric ordered, and the queen set two small glasses with ice on the bar and filled them with cola from a soda gun. Lyric picked up our drinks and turned. "Let's go on to the back."

The place was more crowded than it first appeared. All the tables were full, and on a small stage, a dancer made indecent moves around a pole. Closer, she appeared young and wholesome. She had a little fat around her waist. I wondered if she would take off the skimpy, sequined patch that barely covered the area between her legs. She didn't. Her nipples were barely covered by a sparkling, rosy-pink, push-up bra. Her straight dark hair hung over her shoulders and just missed covering those breasts.

Standing against the wall, we watched until the song ended, and she stepped down from the stage while another girl took her place. She approached Lyric and put her arms around him. When she let go, I could see her face was covered with sweat and running makeup. She was panting from exertion. Lyric introduced us; the dancer was Bobbie Bobbins. I stuck out my hand to shake and told her I was Jeannie.

In a deep, resonant bass voice, Bobbie said, "Charmed, I'm sure." She asked for a cigarette, and

Lyric held out his almost empty pack. She didn't look like she wanted to converse. Closer to her, I could see her beautiful dark hair was a wig, a good one that looked like her own God-given hair from the stage. Then I saw her Adam's apple. My eighteen-year-old knowledge of the world told me that females didn't have them. I glanced at her glistening bra again. Her breasts, I now understood, were an illusion, appearing small but real.

Bobbie said, "I've got to sit down and rest before the next show," and with that, she did a Serena Williams twirl and moved away from us.

I turned around and raised my voice enough to be heard over the music.

"He seemed nice."

"You mean *she*."

"She is a he, isn't he?"

"At one time. But when a guy is dressed as a female, we call him she, no matter how unconvincing she looks."

"Are they trans?" I was curious. I'd never seen a cross-dresser up close before.

"The dancers? No. Drag queens dress up for shows. Transgender individuals dress like the sex they feel they are rather than the one they're born with. Trans people usually take hormones to change their bodies, and often have some kind of surgery."

"But were Bobbie's breasts altered in some way?"

Lyric turned to me, appearing somewhat annoyed.

I apologized immediately.

He smiled and slid his arm around my waist. "Sometime soon we'll have a long talk about it."

The music started again, and another girl climbed

onto the stage, replacing the girl who had replaced Bobbie. We both set our empty glasses on the bar and left. I found myself wondering if Lyric was gay. With the exception of the snake up the back of his head, he had an androgynous appearance.

Lyric said, "Could you eat something?"

"What?"

"The hamburgers next door are pretty good."

I'd smelled the things since the far side of the rear parking lot. "Why not?"

I followed him into the tiny burger place. The counter was full, every seat taken, and some folks were standing. A couple was in line ahead of us. Lyric stepped up to the cash register. The woman there seemed to know him. He motioned toward me. I hoped he hadn't gotten us ahead of the couple who was there first. When I got close enough to hear him, he said, "We're getting them to go."

I dug the twenty out of my pocket and held it out. "I'll get the check this time."

Lyric didn't argue.

Outside again, we found a bench. Lyric passed me the change from the twenty, then unpacked the brown paper bag. We had canned cola and a burger each. I started taking the wax paper off mine.

"Be careful," Lyric said. "They're juicy."

As he said it, I felt warm grease run between my fingers. I held the burger away from me until it stopped dripping. Part of it was still wrapped when I bit in.

We sat for a while, watching people come and go from one place and then the next. The wind off the water was cold. I thought about the pole dancer again. I was trying to get it to fit in my knowledge about such things, so I asked, "Are there more men who want to be women than women that want to be men?"

A group of people passed us, laughing and arguing. I was distracted trying to figure out their genders. I'd forgotten my question, but Lyric hadn't.

He said, "Neither. I think it's about equal. It just seems like there are more men because men who dress like or transition into women have everything going against them. They can take hormones, grow breasts, and whatnot, but they'll still wear size 13D shoes, have broad shoulders, large hands, and an Adam's apple, and all of that is hard to hide. So they're easier to recognize."

I quit then. I would later realize that questions like this opened Pandora's box.

The wind picked up, and a furious gust blew my hair over my shoulders and into my face. I yelped and reached to pull it back. Lyric held his hand out to me, and I saw a black ball cap.

"Thanks," I said, tugging my hair out of my eyes, twisting it, and pulling the cap down.

"Bring one when you come down here at night. You can't see those wind gusts coming. Sometimes it feels like they might knock you off your feet." He tilted his head. "That one looks nice on you. Keep it."

"Thanks. I can pay you."

"Don't. I want you to have it."

The next morning, I picked up the cap and read the letters. *Seminoles for Sobriety*. I would later learn that Lyric's father was half Native American and one hundred percent recovering alcoholic. I asked Lyric if I could ask his father if he ever saw my mother at meetings. Lyric explained that AA has these traditions. One is anonymity. "Who you see here, what you hear here, when you leave here, let it stay here. He can't tell you if she's there or not."

Truth was, just living with her told me the answer. If she went to meetings, she was struggling.

Lyric chewed his last bite and swallowed. Then he said, "What's the deal with your mom? Why are you with your grandma instead of her? Why haven't you been with her all this time?"

"Long story."

"Come on. We've got three hours left before my dad gets home. It can't be that long."

After all my questions, he certainly had the right to ask one of his own. But this was personal. Finally, I sighed and said, "The short story is that she abandoned me when I was ten years old."

"Uh. Sorry."

"Thanks." For some reason, I wanted to tell him the whole story—not just the short version. So I began, "My father came home to live with us the day before she left. He'd been in prison for helping rob a bank. A security guard was killed, not by him, but all four of them got long sentences. Day after he came home, my mother left without a word. Then Dad and I lived alone together for almost five years until he was killed by one of his robbery partners. After that, I went to my grandma's house to live."

Lyric took a cigarette from his shirt pocket and offered me one.

I shook my head.

He patted his pocket for a lighter and lit his. Finally, he said, "What a tragic life."

It didn't seem to me that I had a tragic life. I'd had some big losses. I'd learned to love and learned to lose—well, maybe not lose Legs yet. When those words went through my mind, they sounded corny. Maybe

I'd learned those things a little early, but it seemed to me that everybody learned them—corny or not.

He shrugged. "Are you glad you and your mom reconnected?"

"I'm not sure." I tried to go on with the story without showing my agitation. "I'll probably stay with Grandma until I'm out of high school, maybe out of college. I don't mind, I've come to love her a lot. She's the one steady thing in my life. Until a few days ago, I had a lover, a basketball girlfriend. She's so beautiful, tall, with short blond hair. Now I don't know if I have her or not."

"You've got something going in the looks department," Lyric said casually. "You're young. If you want to, you'll find another woman or a man or whatever you're looking for."

"Thanks." I blushed. Then to make things clear, I blurted, "Legs and I were lovers. When she told me she was leaving, she took the top layer of skin off my heart."

We were quiet for a moment. Maybe I'd been a little overdramatic. But I felt like she'd hurt me something awful.

Finally, Lyric asked, "Have you ever had a boyfriend?"

"No, nor have I been tempted." Later, I wondered if it was an appropriate question. And much later, I felt it was.

Three young people went into the tattoo parlor. Another two waited outside and finally disappeared between the buildings where the walkway led to the parking lot.

Lyric was quiet. Then he asked, "So where does that leave you? Why are you here?"

"When I broke up with Legs, I wanted to get away for a couple of weeks."

"Seems like you're still involved with her."

I nodded. A perceptive observation.

Another gust tugged at the bill of my cap. I was cold and wanted to go home. I wanted to be sleeping on the back porch at Grandma's. I wanted her and Diablo. I wanted Ruthie. I especially wanted Legs. I turned and looked out at the dark water. The wind blew a tear from my eye back toward my ear.

"This is nice," I said to Lyric, even though I'd started to shiver.

"You're freezing. We should go."

"I can't see the ocean, but I can smell and hear it. It's peaceful in a way."

"You should see it at dusk," Lyric said. "The waves come in and deposit sand and seaweed on the beach, and when the current goes out, it takes sand that was already there with it, and the beach is never the same again. To a lesser degree, I think that our lives operate like that, too."

"What?"

"This may sound hackneyed. Everybody we meet, or even see, changes us a bit. When we love, the ebbing current takes everything."

"You're waxing philosophical."

I wasn't sure he understood me.

But he went on, "In a bar in Key Largo, I heard my mom tell the dishwasher Haley that we love who we love. The facts are irrelevant. A person could be perfect, and we'd find him boring. A person could have an eighth-grade education and hate dogs, but we could want him with every cell of our body. You can't tell me people don't change us like the waves change the beach. We change, but who we want doesn't change."

Was he saying that I loved Legs to the exclusion of all others because of some screwy trick my heart played on me? That I would turn down the best woman in the world because my heart wanted what it wanted? I remembered Emily Dickinson, who Joyce fussed at me about her original, "The heart wants what it wants, or else it does not care." God, I loved Legs. I loved her so much it frightened me. I wanted her to know that I was in pain. I wanted her to hurt, too.

But why did I want the person I love in pain? Look at all I'd done to keep her, and it would probably drive her further away from me. I sighed and said, "I'm cold, but I hate to leave." I didn't know how I'd stand to go back to my mother's and wait there alone.

He pointed over my shoulder. "Look there, then we'll leave." The moon was rising behind the end of the pier. The lights were still on. People, perhaps lovers, were walking hand-in -hand out to where a merry-go-round and a bait shop were still doing business.

Lyric held out his hand. "Come on. We can do this again." I let him guide me between the buildings. As we got to the gravel of the parking lot, Lyric said, "Did you see that?"

"What?"

"Those two guys behind Magnolia's."

I started to turn around, but he stopped me.

"Don't. They're back there tricking."

"Is that what it's called?" I didn't wait for an answer. "You're kidding, right out in the open?"

"In a shadow. Sometimes gay guys and straight guys too come into the bar and hook up with someone. Watch the meet rack next time we're in there. Those guys are looking to find someone."

"That's sad."

"Some gay guys find sex with strangers and what they call 'rough trade' appealing. They want it to the exclusion of a monogamous relationship. Similarly, some guys in relationships trick occasionally."

Even though he'd told me not to, I turned and looked. They must have been in a very dark spot because I couldn't see them.

He touched my arm. "If you ever come back to the boardwalk alone, especially at night, take the road around. This shortcut can be dangerous. There have been some clashes. Bashing. Even a murder."

I stopped walking. "What do you mean a murder?"

"Just what I said. I maintain it was one of the straight guys who come in to harass the queens and then somehow hooked up with one of them later. Last winter, a popular entertainer was found dead back here. He'd been strangled."

"By a straight man?" I asked, a bit surprised.

Lyric shrugged and went back to his story. "Police didn't investigate. Some of Magnolia's patrons tried to look into it. They came up against a brick wall. Nobody cares if some drag queen gets killed. Even a famous one. Some people think he deserved it.

"There should have been forensic testing. The person who found the body swore there was semen all over the place. Even fingerprints got lost in the shuffle. We waited for something to come of that. Nothing ever did."

"I'm sorry." What else could I say?

Lyric stopped walking and took me by the arm. "Just promise me, if you ever come down here alone at night, take the long road around. You'll be safe, and

I won't have to worry about a guest of Florida getting killed."

I promised.

"Good. Thank you."

During the short walk home, we were quiet. I had a thousand questions, but there didn't seem to be much time for them.

When we first met at the pool that morning, his slender body, gentle gestures, beautiful eyes, and his voice had seemed a little feminine, and now his knowledge of the LGBT community made me want to ask him if he'd ever been with a boy, the way he had asked me, but I decided to wait. I'd have plenty of time, I thought.

So the question, "Was he gay?" rattled around in my brain for a while. I wasn't sure why I wanted to know. Maybe because I was a lesbian, and we would be of the same breed—with no hope of a love/sex relationship. Then I could relax with no worry of there being more to deal with.

I supposed there were lots of windows to sexuality. Lots of gray areas. So if straight were white and gay were black, I thought I'd fall at charcoal gray. There was little chance I'd want to be close sexually with any male. But Lyric hadn't suggested anything like that. Now that I knew about a murder, my mind went there. I couldn't stop focusing on it.

That first night, what Lyric told me about the murder was upsetting. Not that a dead man wasn't upsetting enough, but he'd told me, "The cops turned the murder of an upstanding citizen into a circus. They behaved like the man didn't deserve any respect. He'd died tricking, like a whore."

"Isn't that really how he died?"

Lyric folded his arms across his chest and turned away from me.

"What?"

He looked straight ahead and pounded his words one at a time, like a hammer striking stone. "No matter what the dead man was doing at the time, he didn't deserve to die. But in Florida, hell the whole country, diversity is under attack. Books are being banned, schools have forbidden words and lessons. Decency laws ban male and female impersonation and criminalize drag performances."

My mouth hung open. Certainly, most of us knew about Florida. But we thought that was temporary—the rest of the country was on our side. Now Lyric was telling me that wasn't the case.

Then Lyric said, "Anyway, the murderer might have been, probably was the guy the victim was back there with."

That wasn't the last time we talked about murders in Magnolia's alley. It would happen again and again as another murder occurred and the alley grew more and more dangerous.

We walked across the parking lot and down the street to my mother's house. Both quiet. In our own thoughts. He was still holding my hand when we went through the gate to the backyard. I never was much of a hand holder, but his hand was soft, and I was barely aware of it right then.

We stopped at the kitchen sliding doors. With the keys in my hand, I unlocked the deadbolt.

He said, "Thanks for coming with me. It was fun."

I nodded. "It sure was different. An education."

He pulled me toward him and gave me a modest

hug that I hadn't expected but was glad to get. The thing I missed about the COVID quarantine was hugs. I rarely offered them but was always glad to get one, even though when Grandma found out I was getting illicit hugs, she fussed about it, then in the end started getting her own. We'd lived in fear way too long.

Lyric then turned away and disappeared. I felt a knot in my chest. Why had I told Lyric all that stuff about my life at home? I barely knew him, and it was far too complicated to explain. How could I ever tell him how it got to be the way it was now? How I ended up living with Grandma and how Legs betrayed me? Most of the time, I wasn't even sure myself. I think he assumed that I was straight or at least not completely gay.

I was tired, the kind of tired that drilled into your bones, where you walk around half comatose. As I crawled into bed that night, I hung Lyric's ball cap on the bedpost, pulled a cover over my head, and closed my eyes.

Wonderful, I know three people in Florida. One is my neighbor who, despite the obvious, thinks I'm straight, one is my mother who is never here, and one is the old lady across the street, who held a gun on me.

The cool ocean air had made me sleepy. I curled up. Later, I was awakened by the sounds of someone opening the kitchen sliders. Then her purse and keys hit the breakfast table. Although I hadn't expected her, Mom had come home. I heard her crack open my door to check on me. I slept again. Sometime later, I rolled over and opened my eyes. A little stream of light made by the moon outside my window crossed my bedroom floor. The same moon that had risen over the end of the pier. Over the merry-go-round and bait shop.

Chapter Six
(More of Mrs. Boyle)

Early the next morning, Lyric came to the door to ask if I wanted to come out while he swam laps. Keep him company, he called it.

I yawned and rubbed my eyes.

"Did I get you out of bed?" he asked.

Although I couldn't think of a reason, I told him I needed to get up anyway.

"So you wanna get in the pool this morning?"

"Sure."

Inside, I pulled my new suit from the bag, ripped off the tags, and found it a good fit. Although it made me look like I was thirty years old, I found things to like about it. For example, the light blue flowers against a navy blue background were sort of pretty. Then the ruffles across the top camouflaged my small breasts. I checked the burn on my nose and found it a little lighter.

Lyric had already skimmed the pool, and the water was rippling azure. I floated in an area away from his splashing and found it relaxing. Trying to swim a couple of laps alongside him was exhausting. I told him I was going to try to finish the night's sleep. He gave me a half salute, and I went in. I threw my wet suit on the shower floor. I would never behave this way at Grandma's. There we all shared one bathroom. Anyway, my mother didn't care.

❧❧❧❧

Later, I was awakened by the doorbell. I pulled a shirt down over my head, and while walking and skipping, I stepped into my gym shorts and pulled up the elastic waist. The bell rang again, so without a thought, I pulled the door open. There stood Mrs. Boyle.

"My goodness," she said. "What happened to your nose?"

Early that morning, before I lay back down, I'd covered my nose with gauze and tape. Even though I could see the white bandage if I crossed my eyes, I'd forgotten about it. I reached for it, and Mrs. Boyle said, "Leave it be. It's just the sun, right?"

Hot air was coming in. "What time is it?"

She shrugged. "Too late to be in bed."

I asked myself what I should do—let a crazy woman in or let the cold air out. I considered slamming the door in her face and hiding out until my mother came home. But in the end, after looking her up and down and seeing no gun, I stepped back and asked her inside.

She kept talking. "I come because I just got back from the store, and I know you're here alone. So why don't you come over to my house for lunch?" She waited for an answer and receiving none said, "Please come. I don't think we got off on the right foot. We can get to know each other."

I didn't really want lunch or to get to know her, but I had to agree that getting pinned down by a rifle was not a good start. I tried one last time. "I just got out of bed."

I was sure she wouldn't accept it, and she didn't.

"You did come in late last night."

Why did her knowing that not surprise me? Lyric and even my mom had told me about her. "I was in the pool this morning, and my skin is covered in chlorine. I need to shower and get dressed."

"I'll watch the News at Noon while I wait." She picked the remote up and plopped down on the couch. A spring protested as she flipped channels until she found *Leave it to Beaver*. She set the remote on the coffee table and picked up the latest *People* magazine.

I left her to it. In the kitchen looking for something to drink, I remembered Mom had made a fresh pot of coffee, which due to the automatic shutoff, was cold. She'd left Pop-Tarts on the counter next to the coffeepot, and tacked to the fridge was a note that said, "Drink the milk." She probably thought I'd be up before noon, but last night at Magnolia's and the early morning swim had worn me out. I didn't really want milk but poured some.

Mrs. Boyle called from the living room, "Are you finding plenty to fill your time?"

I shrugged. "Lyric is helpful."

"He's a good boy."

Clothes were scattered on my bedroom floor. Stepping over what was there, I made my way to the shower, hung my swimsuit over the shower rod, then hastily washed and rinsed my hair, and soaped and cleaned the rest of my body. Back in the bedroom, I put on cutoff jeans and looked for a T-shirt. I'd noticed women of my shape didn't always wear bras. So I slid my worn-out, gray NBA Derrick Rose T-shirt, with the neck cut out, over my head and stepped into my flip-flops.

Before we left Mom's house, I pulled the gauze

off my nose, tossed it in the trash, then checked the bathroom mirror. I was surprised to see it looked a little better. Less red, anyway. I must admit, I did feel better cleaned up. I found myself hungry for whatever Mrs. Boyle was serving.

I followed her across the street with a quick step. The heat made waves from the pavement. All was quiet. For her age, she moved quickly. She opened her front door and held it for me. Stepping into her house, I noticed the air was cold, and it smelled like a combination of jasmine and mothballs. A window air conditioner hummed in the living room. It did a good job cooling the combined area of the living room and dining room. Green plants in front of a window hid the torrid sunlight. It was the type of place where time seemed to move slowly. Perfect for an old lady.

Mrs. Boyle said, "Rose isn't with the Bulls anymore."

At first, the comment seemed to come from nowhere. Then I looked down at my shirt, a little surprised that she knew the name of the one-time Chicago golden child, who became a disappointing point guard for the Knicks due to one injury after the next, and most recently played off the bench for the Grizzlies. "It's an old T-shirt. At the time, I thought he'd be with Chicago forever. I think he thought that, too."

"Funny how life can turn on a dime. One day, everything is going well, and next, you have a president assassinated, 9/11 attacks, a hurricane that floods New Orleans, a pandemic, or any number of events that change our lives forever."

"Rose's story is comparatively small next to those things." My life with Legs had been changed forever.

I wasn't even sure what it would look like after this summer, which scared me.

But we wouldn't talk about basketball, my life, or much larger things, at least not at that time. Instead, she said, "Help me get these things on the table."

The dining room table was full of nonfood items: a stack of newspapers and another of magazines, and a napkin holder that held a bunch of odds and ends—everything except napkins. That was where my grandma kept her unpaid bills. There wasn't much of the tablecloth to be seen. It reminded me of the first time I saw Grandma's dining room table. I'd eaten there often, but at those times, she must have cleaned beforehand because the day I moved in, I'd seen it for what it was—a messy catchall. However, Mrs. Boyle had no cat, while Grandma's cat slept in the center of it all. I'd gotten used to Grandma's table, so Mrs. Boyle's table made me feel a little homesick.

I put a tray of bread, bologna, sliced cheese, mustard, and mayonnaise in the center of the huge table on top of a level stack of magazines. She followed me with paper plates and silverware. And when she saw the food tray on top of the magazines, she smiled. "Iced tea or ice water?"

"I'll have what you're having."

She went back to the kitchen and returned with a sweaty pitcher of tea and two tall plastic glasses.

I poured for both of us.

She said, "I hope you don't mind lunch meat."

I sat with one leg crossed beneath me on a padded chair. If Mrs. Boyle noticed, she didn't mention it.

I said, "Actually, I was getting hungry. Bologna is perfect. Thanks."

Next to me in the dining room corner, she had

three tall antique glass-fronted china cabinets. Two were as tall as me. Glass shelf after shelf of beautiful figurines. I could study them forever and never see them all.

"Dust collectors. That's what my husband used to call them."

"They're beautiful." On one shelf, I saw a complete set of *Wizard of Oz*. Men and women in seventeenth-century formal wear, plus *Gone with the Wind* figurines. Scarlett in the Wilkes barbecue dress with the low bodice. If it hadn't been for Grandma and Joyce, I wouldn't know anything about *Gone with the Wind*, the book or the film. They were both banned because of the racist portrayal of slaves. What would be banned now that gays were under attack?

Mrs. Boyle said, "I enjoy them. I like to handle them and dust them. Sometimes I take them out and set them in circles. When my boys used to play war out under the trees with green army men, I taught them how to set up little battles and dramas. I enjoyed that, too. Wouldn't be able to do it today for my grandchildren, if I had grandchildren, my back and knees give me trouble."

She took four slices of bread and passed the loaf to me. I laid bread on my paper plate. By the time I put bologna, cheese, and mustard on them, Mrs. Boyle was eating. While I worked on my sandwich, I thought about how I'd been hijacked right out of my bed, into this room, and this meal. But I was having a good time.

She passed a bag of potato chips to me. "Get you some of those sweet pickles. They're good."

"Thanks, I'll fill up without them."

She crunched on a bite and smiled. "So tell me, honey, where have you been all this time?"

"I've been living in a little town near Chicago with my grandma."

"Why didn't you come live with your mother?"

I shrugged and then forced myself to say, "I'd rather not talk about it."

"Oh. Oh, sure. I didn't mean to pry."

Nervously, I reached for a cold pickle and took a crunchy bite with my front teeth. Then, I went for another. They were good. After swallowing the second pickle, I pushed the jar back over the table to her. Then I asked, "You always lived here alone?" I remembered after my question that she'd just told me about her husband and sons. Obviously, she hadn't always been alone.

She shook her head right away. "I've been here almost forty years. At first, there were four of us. My husband died of lung cancer in ninety-five. We had our problems, but I can't think of a man I'd have wanted more. I lost my oldest, Larry, to the Iraq war almost ten years later. Wasn't that the one that Bush made up? No one ever told me. How can you send a son away to fight some made-up war and never see him again? Anyway, that left me and my youngest boy alone here, and eventually, my youngest took to drinking, and we constantly quarreled, leading to him moving into a little apartment in town. Strange thing is, I was hard on him because I didn't want to lose him, but my need for peace drove him out. He calls on my birthday and so on. I know he's there if I need him."

I sighed and said, "Family." I was thinking of my own, but Mrs. Boyle took it as a sympathetic sigh.

"You homesick yet?"

I nodded. "A little. I'm going to try to call my grandma this afternoon. We've been playing phone tag."

"Close to your grandma, are you?"

"Yeah. When I was a kid, living with my mother, I hated Grandma because Mom hated her. Mom left the day after Dad came home. So Dad raised me, from age ten till I was fifteen. I got closer to Grandma then. Dad and I were poor right after Mom left. We went to Grandma's for meals and so on. She's never been a good cook, but it was food. Then my dad died. I had to live with Grandma or go into foster care. I chose Grandma, figuring I would just stand it until I was old enough to leave. But Grandma won me over."

"Where had your dad been?"

"Huh?"

"You said your mom left the day after your dad came home. Where had he been?"

I took a bite of my sandwich, trying to decide if I wanted to go into it. Then I swallowed and said, "Prison. When Dad got out, I was ten years old and had never met him. Right away, Mom up and left me with a man I didn't even know." Suddenly, I realized I'd gone too far. Mrs. Boyle knew my mom. I didn't want her to think badly of her.

"How did that go?"

I hesitated and then went on. "It was wonderful. We got along well. He was a good dad. The grandma I live with is his mother."

"So your mother was out of the picture? How did you end up here then?"

"We reconnected when she came to my father's memorial. She said she wanted me to live with her. I refused. It took a long time to even get to where we could talk. But she worked at it. So here I am, visiting for a few weeks."

"So you decided to give her a chance?"

I sighed, thinking I'd already told her more than I wanted. Would she text this stuff all over the neighborhood? Finally, I said, "I don't want to talk about this stuff anymore. Tell me about your sons." I thought that was a clever diversion. Turns out, it was.

She started with, "Those boys never got along. Larry played football. Dana was quiet and artistic. They were only two years apart. You'd think they would play together once in a while. But they grew up at odds with each other. Larry went into the service thinking he'd get a college education. And he would have, had he not been killed in Iraq. Dana was more creative. But in the end, he started drinking and staying out half the night. It was all I could do to get him to finish high school. I finally had enough of his drunken behavior and asked him to get his own place. He was twenty. Old enough. So that's how it stands with him. The thing is, after he was on his own, he had to get a job to pay his rent, and to keep a job, he had to quit drinking every night. So the very thing I agonized about probably saved his life. It's been several years. He owns his own business these days. I'm proud of him." She quickly followed all of this with, "Now would you like a piece of cake?"

In my imagination, I could see Mrs. Boyle as a short, plump angel with a lavender halo. Cake was the perfect thing. "Yes." I was sure I would gain a few pounds, but I couldn't resist. We were both tired of talking about our lives. The cake topped it off. Later, I'd wonder how it had been so easy to talk to her about my history.

"Got a chocolate cake at the store. Don't usually keep it around. If I did, I'd eat it all and end up in a diabetic coma."

I laughed. Well, it was funny! Then I quickly finished what little I had left of my sandwich and chips. She set a paper plate in front of me with a huge slice of chocolate layer cake. She then set her own serving down across from me and picked up her fork. At last, we ate quietly.

She was scraping the icing off her plate when she said, "You come back any time you want. The older I get, the fewer friends I have. I read somewhere that a good social life keeps your brain functioning. I'm somewhat forgetful, but my doctor tells me it's normal for my age. No Alzheimer's."

"Thank you. My grandma has a wife and doesn't suffer loneliness the way some of her friends do. She's also had some friends pass on these last few years."

"They didn't pass on."

Well, I was darn sure they did. "What do you mean?"

"I prefer the word die. It's what really happened. My husband died. My son Larry died. Where the hell did they go if they passed?"

I understood.

She went on, "Old folks eventually get too senile to live alone and get out to visit. Miss Pratt was my bingo friend. Then she set her kitchen on fire and accidentally killed her cat. She got put in assisted living. I went to see her at first, but eventually, it didn't seem to matter. She didn't know me. Miss Pratt made a fuss about her cat. Now she doesn't remember his name."

I was half listening, half looking at the remaining cake. She noticed and told me to take more. I reached for the plate.

"Cut me one, too." She slid her paper plate

toward me.

As I forked a final big piece of chocolate icing, Mrs. Boyle pulled out a menthol cigarette and offered one to me. Without a thought, I took it and let her light it with a kitchen match. It was as easy as that: a cool scent of mint penetrated my sinuses. I felt nothing else, not a bit of shame or frustration as I broke a long period of abstinence. I was just happy to have a smoke. Having quit more than two years ago, I often missed them.

We smoked and then astonishingly ate more cake.

Finally, I said, "Listen, I'm alone a lot across the street. If you want company, call me. Call any or all of us. You're a popular lady today."

She gave me a quick smile and started clearing the table.

I helped her clean up and next made to leave. She passed me a Post-it note on my way out the door. "My phone number if you need or want me. Maybe you'll have a need for a crack shot someday."

I laughed and started toward the door, putting the number into my phone.

Mrs. Boyle came up behind me and said, "There are two eggs left in this carton. Take them home so you'll have a hot breakfast when you want one."

I took the carton and thanked her. Then stood there in stunned silence. She knew what I wanted and probably needed. She knew I was eating Pop-Tarts at Mom's.

Thanking her as I left, I noticed her rifle leaning in the corner of her dining room, waiting.

Chapter Seven

When I walked in the door, my telephone chirped with a text from Lyric.

"Did you get any chocolate cake?"

I laughed and texted, "I did." Everyone knew everything around here.

"Good."

He called me then and started with, "I'm going down to the beach this afternoon. Want to come?"

"To do what?"

"Nothing. Breathe the air. Listen to the waves."

"Mom should be home in a few hours."

"Well, just for a few hours then."

"Okay. What should I wear?"

"Long-sleeved T-shirt, jeans, tennis shoes, maybe a sweater. The wind off the water is usually cool this close to the daily storm."

Lyric made Florida worth the trip for me. I enjoyed his company. My visit would be a bust without him. "Meet you out back in ten minutes."

I rushed around my room, digging through my clothes. The temperature was over ninety-five outside. I altered Lyric's list a little and stayed with the cutoff jeans. My NBA T-shirt had Mrs. Boyle's mustard on it, so I went with a plain white tank top, again braless. I grabbed my new sunglasses and stuffed my Seminole ball cap in my back pocket.

Lyric was waiting. He looked me up and down and said, "Looking good today."

"It was the cake."

"See, Boyle's not so bad."

"Except when she pulls a gun on you as a way of introduction."

Lyric laughed. "There is that. But she's a good old girl. Even with a gun in her hands, she means well. She acts a little senile when she thinks her back is against the wall. But she's smart."

"What do you mean, back against the wall?"

"Well, for example, the showdown with the cop. She's not as silly as she sounded."

We walked quietly through the shadows in the alley. The boardwalk was crowded with half-naked people lugging large cold drinks and coolers down closer to the water. Lyric pointed to a spot beyond the pier where surfers came in. I hadn't noticed the little surf shop farther on down, and beyond that was nothing but sand, white caps, and the blue sky.

"You thirsty?"

"I could use a drink," I said, remembering a full glass of milk sitting on the desk in my room.

"We can get something at that surf shop ahead. Drinks are bigger and better there."

I shrugged and said, "Sure," trying to remember if my shorts had money in the pockets.

Ron Don's was crowded with deeply suntanned people in line for drinks or self-serve soft frozen yogurt. Although we weren't one of their numbers, they shifted around and made room for us. A heavy-set guy behind the counter, who could have been Ron Don, took money for drinks, yogurt, rental bikes, and surfboards. He answered questions about his surfing equipment. After a while, I realized he was arguing with a thirteen- or fourteen-year-old boy, who told him his board had been stolen. The kid wanted to make payments on another one. That made sense to me. But the old guy didn't like it.

"'Member that stack out front, three across and four high?"

The boy nodded, obviously unhappy. "Those are old and beat-up. They're all long boards, aren't they?"

"There's three or four shorter ones behind the others. Tell you what, I'll give you a deal on renting one of those. If you return it every night, I'll keep it inside for you. How does five dollars a day sound?"

The boy asked, "Could you make it rent to own?"

Ron Don mopped his big hand over his face, finally saying, "Yes, but if anything happens to it, you pay two hundred dollars to own it. That's a helluva deal, and you know it. Everybody here knows it."

A few people in line turned to watch the negotiation.

Ron Don said, "Those may be used, but they're good boards. I could get over four hundred for any of them. Take it or leave it," and turned away.

The boy dug in his pockets, threw several wadded-up ones and a bunch of change on the counter, and went to pick out his rental.

When we left the surf shop, he was paddling out toward a group of surfers waiting for the next right wave.

We walked on with our cold drinks. Eventually, we came to a couple of wooden benches and a trash can. One seat was totally in the sun, the second caught a little shade from the rising bluffs behind us. A cool wind from the gulf tempered the hot sun. We sat and finished our drinks and took off our shoes. We could see the surfers perfectly—even the boy, who took two spills but did well.

After a while, we walked back to the boardwalk, shoes in our hands, at the water's edge, small waves lapped at our feet.

Lyric said, "I love this. It's the thing I miss about the Keys."

"Lots of shorelines there?"

"Yeah. Though the sand is different. When I'm close to the ocean like this, I feel connected to the world. Like I belong."

I walked next to him for a distance, then I asked, "What do you mean? How is the sand in the Keys different?"

"Sometimes there isn't any sand, just rocks. If little inlets get sanded, people do it. I've seen areas where folks living on the shore would buy sand and spread it along their property. It wouldn't last long because water washes it away. I mean, they were licked before they started. They knew it would happen every time. But they did it anyway."

"My grandma would call those diehards."

I thought he might not be talking about sand anymore and promised myself to think about it later. Right then, the world was beautiful with the blue sky, the sun, and the waves. My heart felt lighter. I hadn't thought about Legs all day. Maybe it would be like that more and more as time passed.

We were quiet for a while. Finally, Lyric stopped and dropped onto the sand. "We need to put on our shoes. There will be rocks from here on."

I wasn't sure where it came from, but I told Lyric, "I won't stay with my mom much longer. I'm going back home." This was still in my first week.

"When?"

"Dunno. Soon. The longest I'll stay is two more weeks."

"You don't have to go so soon."

"No. But I want to."

⁂

The hot sun was streaming through my bedroom window the next morning, and my phone was ringing. I found it under yesterday's underpants. Grabbing it, I curled up again. It was early even for Grandma. I mumbled, "Mm-hmm." I must have nodded off because my phone chirped again. I grabbed it and said, "Hello."

"Jeannie? Did you hang up?" I recognized Grandma's voice. "That you?"

"Grandma, it's me. Still sleepy. I'm so glad we finally connected."

"I've been calling. Joyce says we should get one of those cellphones so I can text. I still refuse."

I laughed. "Don't ever change." I hadn't talked to her for five days, way too long for me.

"Have you made any new friends since you got there?"

"I have. There's a neighbor boy who comes over to use the pool. He's my age. We get along all right. An old lady across the street had me over for lunch." I didn't dare tell Grandma about the rifle. She might not have seen the humor, if there had been humor.

"A boy," she said. "Is he a friend or maybe something more?"

"Oh, Grandma, he's cute, but I don't think more than a good friendship will come of it."

"Can't have too many good friendships." She

cleared her throat and said, "Just remember, I was with your grandpa for three years. I was happy enough. We had two children. Sexuality is full of possibilities."

I shook my head to clear it. I couldn't believe she'd said that to me. "How did that work, you being a lesbian and all?" I asked in a surly tone.

Grandma went on like she hadn't heard me. "There was a war. We cared for each other. I might have been with him longer if he had survived Vietnam. When I was alone, a widow, I started up with women. All kinds of things can happen."

"Right."

"You know this story," she said.

"Yes. But Lyric and I are friends. We hang out together. I just lost Legs. It's too soon for anyone else. Plus, I'm a lesbian. I've known that since the first time Legs kissed me. Probably longer. I've envied you and Joyce. That's what I want someday."

"Okay. You don't have to convince me. Without you here, my mind runs amok."

"My sexual preference is the one thing in my life that's stable. I won't screw it up by taking up with a boy. Besides, I think he's gay." I was getting a headache and wondered what time it was.

Here I was, gearing up for a heated discussion, and Grandma changed the subject. "So how is it going with you and your mother?"

I hesitated and then told her, "She seems to be trying. I am, too. She got me a Slipknot T-shirt. I wear it everywhere, but she's not always here to see it."

"She gone a lot?"

"Yes. She has the same boyfriend since the last time we saw her. His name is Charlie. He drives a truck, and when he's in town, she's with him a lot."

"Why don't the three of you do something?"

"I think she knows how I feel about him. In fact, I all but told her I would not want him here overnight. You remember him, don't you? He was with her when she came to Dad's memorial."

"The guy who came into the men's room to find you?"

I laughed. It wasn't long until four women were in the men's room, and Charlie had escaped somewhere. I was angry with Mom and him after that. My father was dead. I had enough to deal with. I didn't need to be stalked by the mother who abandoned me and the date she brought.

"So," Grandma said, "they've been together all this time. Maybe Alberta is settling down."

"Maybe. I just don't care for him. Something about the way he acts and the way he treats her bothers me. I don't want him staying here. Plus, the things she does with him don't support the way she told me she was living."

"What do you mean?" Grandma asked.

"She carries a beer around whenever she's going with him."

"Why don't you come home? We miss you. Diablo misses you. You don't have to stay all summer."

"I feel like I have to stay a little longer. How is Legs? Has she left for Miami?" My heart leapt when I said her name.

Grandma hesitated. Finally, she said, "Legs left last Sunday night."

"Why didn't you tell me?" I was angry. I'd wanted to know about what she was doing, so I could keep my dreams about her real—if dreams were ever real.

Grandma said, "You can't leave her and hang on

to her both. I think she cared a great deal for you. But you left. It was your choice." As if to say something kind or reassuring, Grandma added, "There will be others. You're young and just starting out."

"Did she seem happy?" To be honest, I wanted her to be as miserable as I was. Once, my father told me the things most people wanted from life were work they loved and a person they looked forward to coming home to after work. I had neither.

"Sure," Grandma said. "Everyone was there, her foster family, me and Joyce, and some kids from school. I think Ruthie was there."

I remembered how attracted to Legs Ruthie had been in the beginning. She wanted her for herself. But it hadn't worked out that way. I sighed. Sunlight streamed across my bed, across my legs. The room was too warm, I was sweating, and a headache was starting.

Grandma's voice grew tender. "You could have been there Monday night, but you broke up with her. You ran away. Everything you do or don't do has consequences, Jeannie." When she said my name, she sounded hundreds of miles away, which she was.

I didn't like being told that I'd run away, but it was true. "I know. Being here made me realize how much I care for her."

"You're learning."

Neither of us said anything for a moment. Then Grandma said, "Joyce and I thought we'd send something. Is there anything you want or need?"

"Nothing." I was still thinking about Legs. "Alberta bought me a swimsuit, sunglasses, and a Slipknot T-shirt."

"Okay, money then." Next, she said, "You haven't asked about Joyce, but she fell off a ladder and broke her left wrist."

"Oh, no, how did that happen?"

"The cat got out. The neighbor's German shepherd was loose. Diablo and he were growling at each other. Then the cat ran right up from the front porch to the roof. When Tigger gets on the roof, she never can get down by herself. Joyce had to get the ladder. They were almost down when Joyce missed a rung and fell."

"Is it painful?"

"You know Joyce. She wouldn't complain if she were hurting. The doctor put her in a cast, so she's been curled up on the couch with one of her Virginia Woolf novels."

"Are you serious?" I could see her on that couch. It sagged in the middle and was a foot too short for an adult.

"Yep."

"Where'd she find another Virginia Woolf?" I knew they weren't cheap at the bookstore.

"Church garage sale. She bought several of those books. She's such an egghead."

"I suppose if you have to be down, reading something you love, especially while lying on the couch, sounds like good medicine."

Grandma said, "I suppose. No one understands Joyce like you. Not even me."

That gave me a warm feeling. I didn't understand Virginia Woolf, but hours of lying around reading sounded splendid. I understood that much about Joyce, and it seemed to please Grandma, who read mostly lesbian mysteries.

Grandma said, "Listen, I've got to go. Since you don't need anything, we'll send you money. Use it if you find something you want or for your ticket home. Just let us know when you're coming so we can pick you up."

We declared our love for each other and hung up.

I tried to go back to sleep, but it was hopeless. I was upset about Legs, and I was homesick. My mind jumped from Legs to Joyce to Diablo and home. There I was in a strange bed, in a strange room with a headache. Even with the Slipknot T-shirt, my life felt empty. Talking to Grandma made me feel alone.

I got up and headed to the bathroom. I'd slept in my underpants, and when I passed the mirror, I noticed a pooch in my belly. I wondered how much weight I'd gained in the few days I'd been in Florida on a steady diet of Pop-Tarts, chocolate cake, and pizza. I hadn't worried about weight since I was a kid and Dad took over caring for and feeding me. Damn.

I pulled a T-shirt down over my head and went into the kitchen. I was pretty sure that coffee would help the headache. I poured a cup and put it in the microwave.

Thinking about Legs, I couldn't imagine my life without her. I was going to call her. I wanted to say I was sorry, and I wanted to work things out.

Chapter Eight

The following week, on a hot day, as we strolled down the beach toward the surf shop, Lyric broached the subject of girlfriends present and past. I was happy for the chance to talk about Legs; I missed her so much. After that, he'd know for sure that I was a lesbian looking only for friendship from him. I'd heard of straight boys thinking they could convert lesbians. We were both young enough that some sexual experiences might be unknown to us—at least that was what I thought. From my viewpoint, there were two kinds of people—straight and gay. Yet when I was laid up with a broken leg, I searched Joyce's books for more to read, and there I found a biography of Pauli Murray, which opened up more about sexuality to me. A woman could live as a lesbian, but in bed, she might want to be the male.

After our first time at Magnolia's, Lyric tried to explain drag queens from trans men and women. I didn't think he'd be horrified about my lesbianism because he was so relaxed at Magnolia's. What was more, I'd suspected that he was gay since the day we met. I was sure the story he was about to tell me was about a male lover. But that wasn't how it went.

***

I told him, "My father died in the autumn three and a half years ago, and I moved in with my grandma.

That's when I found Legs living across the alley. We both played on the high school basketball team. I played shooting guard and sometimes point, and Legs was our sixth man and center. It wasn't long until we were in love."

Then I stopped, holding back something like beginning tears.

Lyric watched me, then touched my shoulder. "How old were you when your dad died?"

"Fifteen. He was murdered."

"God! You don't have to go on if you don't want to."

I swallowed. "I'm fine. Those tears sneak up on me when I least expect them. Anyway, Grandma and I had him cremated. It was a choice forced by finances." I added that when I explained the beginning with Legs to Lyric. I thought it was important.

He'd nodded. "People like us are familiar with big things being determined by money, or lack thereof."

I stared out at the clear sky, the ocean, and the clear horizon and started talking again. "Anyway, later that winter, we held a memorial service at my friend Ruthie's church. Between Grandma's people, my school and basketball friends, as well as everyone who knew my father and what a good man he was, the place was filled to the brim.

"When the evening was over, one that included a visit from my absent till then mother and her boyfriend, Charlie, I was frazzled. Legs and I were sitting on the steps while the last stragglers came out of the church and Grandma could lock up. She was telling me about a 'friends with benefits' arrangement she had with a girl named Malu who she brought to a school dance. To be honest, I brought it up. I'd seen her with the girl and asked her if she thought about living with Malu someday. That was when Legs told me that if she had a girlfriend like me, she'd never want another thing. I held her to that right till the last time I saw her."

Lyric said, "If you asked about Malu, you must have been, in some way, interested in Legs."

I nodded. "My grandma is a lesbian, and I'd had thoughts in that direction since I was thirteen or fourteen while my father was still alive. I didn't investigate those feelings. Now and then, a boy looked good to me. Then I met Legs."

At this point, Lyric interrupted me and said I looked straight to him. I still wasn't sure how I felt about that. My hair was shoulder length. I wore it that way because my dad liked it. I thought the way I dressed might give me away. But at school, lots of girls dressed in flannel shirts and jeans. However, when I became Legs's girlfriend, I was marked. It was that night, after Dad's memorial, Legs let me know how powerful her attraction to me was.

"A couple of weeks later, she walked me home, right to my back door. On impulse, I threw my arms around her and planted a kiss on her lips. In addition to surprising her, I turned around, and there were Grandma and Joyce, watching us. Legs pointed out that now I didn't have to come out to them."

Lyric had listened to me while we walked. Describing our first kiss made him laugh. When my story was over, I waited for him.

At last, he said, "Not long ago, most gay kids weren't so lucky to have a funny coming out story. Coming out was usually full of pain, deceit, and regret."

"Grandma told me it wasn't as bad as it used to

be. Most kids wouldn't be put out in the street these days, but many would be put into conversion therapy."

I sometimes forgot the ways of the world. I knew that kiss was a funny story, and Legs and I laughed about it often. Especially when times were hard, we had some of those, but this summer was the worst.

Lyric and I walked quietly for a while. Ocean water lapped at our feet. We passed a couple of middle-aged people lying under a beach umbrella, each with a beer bottle in hand. About eight kids were laughing and screaming on boogie boards. We stopped and watched them for a few minutes.

I was starting to think that Lyric wouldn't tell his story. But on the way back toward the boardwalk, he told me about the girl he'd been seeing almost since he had moved in with his father.

He cautioned me that he didn't have many funny parts.

Then he said, "I took a job at the bar where my father worked when I first came north. I couldn't drink or serve alcohol because I was seventeen. So I moved things around for them, brought up boxes from the basement, and swept. I worked there after school for as long as I could keep my grades up. I was driving my dad's old rusty Falcon while Dad rode his bike because we came and went at different times. I needed a better car, my own car, so I studied hard to keep those grades up. When things were slow at the bar, I did my homework, sitting in the booth at the back, under the dim barroom light. I avoided my father, and I think he avoided me. On the weekends when we worked together, I was careful to stay out of his way."

I stopped him. "Didn't you tell me you were working mornings at a café?"

"That's for the summer. Tips are good. I still work on the weekends at the bar."

"It's a wonder you have the time to hang out at the beach."

"I have less and less. Anyway, the bar was usually full of bikers on the weekend. I didn't mind it. They tipped well and were good to me. The bikers also got along with each other. If they argued, it was with the women who came with them.

"One night, I was cleaning tabletops when I came upon a pretty woman in the back booth where my homework was packed in a bag ready to carry home. This woman didn't look any older than I was, but it turned out, she was twenty-five. There were wadded-up napkins in front of her. She'd clearly been crying. A warm draft beer was her ticket to the booth. As long as she was still drinking, she was free to take up the room. I said, 'Excuse me. I didn't see you here.'

"She said, 'I'm sorry. This is your homework booth, isn't it?'

"I told her I was finished, but the bar would be closed in twenty minutes. Until then, this booth was hers. Then I asked if I could get her anything else. She shook her head no and said her ride left with another woman and she needed to find a way home. She spent the last of her money on that beer. Then she said she thought her boyfriend left with a blonde.

"I nodded. I didn't know her boyfriend, but the blonde was familiar to me. She hung around the bikers and often left with one or more of them. I didn't know what to say to this woman. She'd been treated poorly. No matter what happened, she shouldn't be left without a way home.

"I finally told her I could give her a ride."

Lyric went on, "I was driving Dad's Falcon, and after closing, I took her to the public housing across town. She lived in one of the second-story units. Her name was Rita, and she had two little kids. The biker friend who abandoned her was not their father.

"She asked if she could repay me for the ride, and I said she didn't have to. I'd been trying to meet new people since I moved here, and I'd count her as new people. But she insisted on cooking dinner for me that Sunday, her day off.

"When she got out of the car, she asked me if I could give her babysitter a ride home. I shrugged and told her I could. A few minutes later, a plump girl with long dark hair came down the steps, opened the car door, and said, 'Hi. I'm Betsy.' Then she got in and told me she lived in the trailer park behind the Walmart.

"She said I looked familiar, and she thought I was in her calculus class. The car was dark, but her profile looked familiar, too. I managed to get her home that night without getting lost.

"You might think that Rita was the heroine of this story. I did go to dinner the next Sunday at her house. She fried a chicken, peeled and mashed potatoes, and roasted corn. I ate so much I thought I'd bust. At home, Dad and I eat mostly processed food, tuna salad, Hamburger Helper, chili from the can, and anything that could be frozen or canned and cooked later. Since we both worked nights, we seldom ate dinner together.

"I thought I might see Rita again. I imagined seducing her. She was old enough for the things I wanted. But by the time I saw her in the bar again, she was with another biker.

"Betsy was in two of my classes: calculus and English 4. I always said 'hello' in class, the hall, and in the lunchroom. Then she did something I found humiliating and exciting at the same time. She bribed the guys who sat next to me in each class and took their seats. Later, she told me that English cost her five dollars and calculus twenty. Seems in calculus, everyone wanted a seat next to someone who understood what was going on. I guess I was one of them.

"After school, I started walking her to her bus. I got to know some of her friends. I wanted a friend. With the bar job, I had one night a week off. So I took her to a movie or out for a hamburger down here on the boardwalk. I worried about where she thought our friendship was headed. It didn't take long to find out. One night, she told me she wanted sex with me. For me, I wanted a friend. I felt that sex would mess that up. Plus, in my mind, she was too young. The laws are kind of screwy in Florida. If someone is sixteen or seventeen, they're at the age of consent if their partner is less than twenty-three years old. Therefore, I couldn't be arrested for having sex with her. I told her how I felt about that, and I could see tears in her eyes. I didn't want to hurt her."

I said, "You seem to know a lot about the laws in Florida."

We stopped walking, and Lyric looked at me for a moment. I realized later that he was debating whether or not he could trust me with more. But then, he shrugged and went on with more about Betsy.

"She told me she was older than most kids in our classes because she was off a semester to have a baby. I stared at her, surprised. Not only was she older than most of our classmates, but she also had a bit of sexual experience.

"I'd known there was a baby in the family but not

that it was hers. She had a son, but the baby's father dumped her long before he was born. The boy's name is Jacy.

"We were alone, usually in the car in front of her trailer when I took her home, and gradually, one time after the next, we started touching. Every time, it became harder to send her inside. One night, I got my hand inside her jeans, and I manipulated her down there until she came. That's when I thought it was over. I hadn't been ready to do that. At that point, I was starting to want her. But I told her we were too young, and if we go on seeing each other, we couldn't do that again.

"Looking back, it was an awful thing to say after that intimacy. But she didn't cry. She squinted at me in anger. She got out of the car and slammed the door, pulling up and zipping her jeans as she went toward the door. Finally, she agreed. It was abstinence or nothing. She did change chairs in English, though."

I asked, "Do you see her now that school's out for the summer?"

"We see each other every now and then. Since I'm working mornings and some nights, our opportunities are fewer. Her eighteenth birthday is coming in July. She's got it in her head, probably because I told her, that the reason for no intimacy is her age."

"So will the reason be gone then?"

"Never. If I had any courage, I'd break it off with her now."

"There's something else, isn't there?"

He turned and looked in my eyes. There was more. Something big he wasn't telling Betsy or me. I thought he was gay from the beginning. He could have—should have—told her.

As we walked on, he was quiet. I could think of a thousand questions. I had been sixteen when Legs first made love to me. In a way, I could see how he was protecting her. But mostly, he was protecting himself.

Chapter Nine

The next afternoon, Lyric told me he was getting another tattoo. The snake on his neck seemed too extreme. He was going to get a poem. Currently working two part-time jobs, he'd been saving his money, and after doing some work in Mrs. Boyle's basement, he decided he had enough.

The sun was still up, and the tattoo artists in the building two doors down from Magnolia's were busy. Lyric had an appointment. There was rarely walk-in business. He told me that people the artist didn't know often waited a month or more to get in.

Lyric's snake coiled from his back and up the side of his neck, behind his left ear, and above where hair would have been if he didn't have it cut nearly off. He wasn't bald, but he wore his light brown hair in a close cut. This time, he wanted a tattoo on his upper leg. Some poem or something.

I had nothing to do but stay home with Mom, who slept late that day because she had to work the evening shift. I tagged along like Scout Finch, the little kid in *To Kill a Mockingbird*, another banned book that I might have never read if it weren't for Joyce. I thought I might want a tattoo myself sometime, so I wandered around the room looking at designs on the wall.

Lyric's artist was a gay guy named Dana, who was covered with tattoos. As he and Lyric talked, I realized I'd seen him in the bar before, not as a dancer but as the lover of the woman with red cheeks like a Russian doll and a tattoo of Janis Joplin on her shoulder. I'd been there a little more than three weeks and was learning the names of Magnolia's patrons. Many of the queens were couples. That gave me hope. I didn't want to spend my life alone or cheat on someone I loved as some of them did. I needed a woman I could trust. Someone who, if she came to the boardwalk, would stay out of the alley. I never met guys in long-term relationships in the bar. One might think monogamous lovers didn't exist, but I was told that many of those guys stayed home and thus stayed away from guys who wanted to trick.

I sat next to Dana to watch him work for a minute before I asked if he cared if I watched. He was starting the third or fourth lines of the poem by then.

"No problem. Maybe you could help."

"How?"

"When you were looking around the shop, did you see any flowers or birds that you liked?"

"Oh, I'm not getting a tattoo for me today."

"It's for this poem," Dana said.

Lyric said, "A small bird singing would be nice."

I stood and crossed the room to a section of birds and looked over each row carefully. I eliminated the flying birds first thing. In the poem, the bird is perched. It seemed like no time at all before Dana called to me, "Got one?"

"I think so."

He stood next to me. I pointed to one with musical notes at the tip of its wings and a treble clef for a body. Dana lifted the bird off the wall and took it back to his workstation to reproduce the picture, and then he tattooed it next to the last word of Lyric's poem.

When Dana was done, he showed me the tattoo. I didn't expect to be too impressed, and I made up my mind to say something nice no matter what it looked like. But there it was, words in script with different shades of blue and green worked in.

Hope is the thing with feathers—
That perches in the soul—
And sings the tune without the words—
And never stops—at all—(then the bird picture)

"I like it," I said. "Where'd you find it?"

"It's Emily Dickinson," Lyric said. "A member of the Math Club I used to run with liked Dickinson a lot."

I wrinkled my nose. "Math Club. Yuck."

He ran his fingers over the new tat gently. I could see he was happy with it. He lowered his gaze a little to meet mine.

I said, "Well, it's beautiful." I meant it. The little musical bird set it off.

Our walk back to Magnolia's was quiet. If the tattoo was painful, Lyric didn't mention it. With pain tolerance, he was like Joyce. She told me once that, to her, physical pain was tolerable. It was emotional pain that was harder to bear. Joyce would have liked the poem and have been able to recognize Emily Dickinson. Something changed in the way I saw Lyric that afternoon. He became a man with a snake tattoo and a brain.

The evening was starting out beautifully. We walked as far as Ron Don's. Ron was sitting next to the open front door on an old kitchen chair, staring out to the horizon where some of his customers waited for a wave to ride. We stopped and bought frozen yogurt in a cone and turned back toward the boardwalk.

When we came to the restaurant where my mother worked, people stood outside the open doors. We watched the sunset with them, its orange hues drifting on the sea. I counted three sailboats and a yacht floating on the skyline. People from the restaurant started wandering back inside to their dinners. The waves came closer to our feet as we walked toward the boardwalk.

At sundown, I could see the lights of Magnolia's. Lyric said, "I'm going to stop for a while and show off my new tattoo. Do you want to come?"

The wind was picking up, and I tugged Lyric's ball cap from my back pocket and pulled it down on my head. I was tired. My day had started with a headache. I decided Lyric might want to be alone with his old friends once in a while. And I wanted to go back to the house. So I said, "I think I'll go home. See you in the morning." When we reached the open door of the bar, he went in, and I went on.

A few minutes later, I jumped down the large step to the space that led between the buildings on the way to the parking lot. It wasn't until I heard voices that I remembered Lyric's warning about coming this way alone. I'd never gone the long way around to the road and wasn't sure about it. We'd watched the sunset from the restaurant. Parts of the alley were light shadows of dusk, but many were dark. I tried to stay in the shadows so no one would know I was there alone.

I heard a man laugh and then moan. The sound came from behind the hamburger joint, near the dumpster. Not the most romantic spot for sex. I decided that the guys would be distracted if I made a sound, plus I would be in the parking lot behind the alleyway before or if they noticed me.

Then I heard a scream, followed by, "Stop it. Get away from me!" A second guy said something. Then another scream and blows thudding on someone's body. I didn't realize that I had started running until I was at the edge of the parking lot. I ran the rest of the way to Mom's house, believing there might be a murderer behind me.

When I got home, I locked the doors and called Lyric. He didn't answer his cell. My heart pounded as I Googled and then called Magnolia's. Loud music and laughter came through in the background as the bartender answered.

It was a few minutes before I heard Lyric's voice.

Breathlessly, I said, "It's me."

"Hi, you change your mind about coming in?

"No. I was walking home and heard something."

"You went through the alley?"

"Yeah. I forgot. Lyric, someone should go out there and check."

"Why?"

"A man screamed."

That was it. He dropped the phone. I heard him calling to someone. I hung up wondering if I should call the cops. I didn't. I stood at the picture window and waited. The flashing lights and sirens passed. I said a prayer and watched first the firetrucks, then the police cars, and last the ambulance. I realized that I had been in that alley with a murderer. I was afraid, but I left the house and walked back down the street toward the alley.

Despite the mist, I saw the emergency vehicles and their revealing lights. As I drew closer, the circling red lights lit up everything. I stood about twenty-five feet from the edge of the parking lot, which was not as full on a weeknight.

Then out of the darkness, like a curtain was opened, Lyric came toward me. "We were too late," he said. "It was Irwin, a part-time bartender. You remember, long, permed red hair, a little on the plump side."

He took my arm and guided me back toward home.

After a moment, I asked, "Was Joe Smith in the bar earlier?"

"Who?"

"He was the guy I met at the airport my first day here. Bobbie Bobbins told me his name the first time I saw him at Magnolia's. Bobbie told me that he tried to seduce Lady Ann more than once. He doesn't belong in Magnolia's, but he's there a lot. I'm sure he's straight. At least he comes in with a bunch of straight guys to watch the shows."

"Might be bi."

"Maybe."

Lyric stopped walking. "You don't need to figure this out. The police will do it."

"But you said they won't." I took a deep breath. "My father was murdered, and it seemed no one was doing anything. My friend Ruthie and I started asking questions. I don't think the guy would have ever been caught if we hadn't." I neglected to tell him that we were almost murdered for our trouble.

Lyric gently took my arm, and we started walking toward home. Finally, he said, "This is too dangerous. If Joe killed these guys, the homicide detectives will figure it out. You and I will stay out of it."

Mom told me what happened the next morning.

She said, "Another gay man was murdered down there. I think you should stay away from that bar."

I couldn't argue with that. But I didn't stay away. Magnolia's was one of the reasons I hadn't left for home yet. I felt comfortable there. I was making friends. It was the only place in the area that had any life in it. I was lonely and couldn't just sit around Mom's all day. Plus, I'd gradually realized that none of those people fit in.

I needed people who didn't fit anywhere else. Truthfully, I was one of them.

While I recognized his description, I didn't know anything about him, so Lyric told me about Irwin, the queen who had been murdered on the night he got his new tattoo. Some said that if it happened to anyone, it would have been him or one of the few like him. Single. A part-time bartender. Heavy drinker. He had slept with several workers, as well as customers. He was usually the first to pick up new meat. He had a reputation for being better at breaking up couples than becoming part of one himself. But that didn't mean he should die.

The cops came up with an excuse to quit investigating. So he had some risky behavior. That was no reason to murder him. Even though the police told us it was, the patrons in the bar didn't think so.

❧ ❧ ❧ ❧

Nearing the Independence Day holiday, there were more people on the boardwalk and shows every night. Straight people, as well as gays, came in. The more performances, the more profit for Magnolia's. The queens got together and put on some elaborate shows. I looked back at it as a time of pleasure in Florida—Lyric and I had fun. I made more new friends. I loved hanging around the bar with a glass of soda in my hands. I ignored Mom's warning and went to the bar with Lyric. And in the late mornings, when Lyric was working a new job and I was lonely, I went alone. I reasoned that if Mom even cared, she had to know I was at the boardwalk.

At night, Lyric and I sat near the stage, laughing with the others. During the torch songs, as Lyric called them, I was often moved to tears. Silly, it was only a man dressed up as a woman lip synching to an old sad song. Judy Garland's *Somewhere Over the Rainbow* got me every time. I was never more aware of my difference from others until I thought about the land over the rainbow. A special place where differences didn't matter. The song made me think of Legs. I told myself there had to be a way to get her back, even if I had to wait a year. She was the love of my life. I don't know where, but I think "love of my life" was a phrase I learned at Magnolia's. I understood it the first time I heard it.

Somewhere Over the Rainbow was Bobbie Bobbins's song. She would stop by our table and help me dry my tears.

"You're too young to be so sad about love," she'd say.

"Trust me," I said. "I'm not. I've already screwed up my first, supposedly permanent romance."

Lyric shared a cigarette with Bobbie, and she would be at our table long enough to soothe me and smoke the damn thing. The tenderness was over once she crushed out her cigarette in the ashtray. After the one I'd smoked with Mrs. Boyle, I'd not had another. I'd smoked since I was very young. I had access to cigarettes as a kid because my mother smoked constantly. All my clothes, as well as my hair, smelled of tobacco. It was hard to avoid helping myself to one of the open and partly smoked packs she kept lying around. After Dad died and I went to live with my grandma, I pilfered her cigarettes. Then one night, I was thinking about my dad, and I found myself promising him I'd quit. And I did pretty much. So I wasn't tempted on those nights Lyric offered his pack to me.

Gradually, I felt like Bobbie had become my friend, more so than the other performers. He sang my song and asked how I was. He even asked how my summer was going. It seemed he took extra time with me. That meant friend to me.

❧❧❧❧

When tourists came into Magnolia's, most of the time, it went well. Now and then, it didn't. Even gays got asked to leave if they were too disruptive. If they started a fight, they would be barred from Magnolia's for a week or so. Straight customers were asked to leave sooner and barred forever. Lady Ann wouldn't tolerate trouble from straights. Occasionally, when they didn't leave—some wanted their cover charge returned, and some wanted to push the queens around—Ivy, from behind the bar, and Lady Ann, the bouncer who collected the cover charge and worked the door, physically took hold and removed them.

One night, I saw the familiar face of the man Bobbie told me was Joe Smith. I knew he was the guy from the airport who I met at the shuttle bench.

When I asked Lyric about him, he shrugged.

"He's just one of the straight guys who comes in late looking for a date. A few of the girls know him. He's rough trade."

By then, I wasn't surprised, but I said, "The girls go with someone like that knowing?"

Lyric said, "Some of them want it that way, if not always then sometimes."

I asked about his name in case Bobbie had been mistaken.

Shoving his hands in his pockets, Lyric said, "Didn't you call him Joe Smith? I guess I could find out for sure if you think it's important." He left me and went over to Lady Ann, and when he returned, he had the name of Joe Smith.

I sighed. "Damn."

"What? You and I are the only people here who use their Christian names. This guy goes by Joe Smith."

I said no more. I didn't want the first person I met in Florida to recognize me, so I stayed as far away from him as I could. Neither Lyric nor the others seemed to notice. Then one night, a shiver traveled down my spine. His gaze met mine and wouldn't tear away. He recognized me. Expressionless, he nodded and then turned away before I could say anything.

❦ ❦ ❦ ❦

I finally got to meet Betsy when she came to Mom's house early in the morning to swim laps with Lyric. Because of Lyric's spoken desire to stop seeing her, I was surprised to find two people in the pool. I didn't know if I should go out there or not. I watched through the kitchen sliders with a cup of coffee in one hand and a Pop-Tart in the other.

Lyric must have been looking for me. If I went out, it was time for me to join him. He came toward the sliders and waved when he saw me.

I swallowed the last of the Pop-Tart and opened the door, coffee in hand.

When Betsy heard the door slide open, her head snapped in my direction. I could see her sizing me up. Maybe she thought I was her competition. That would be my first thought if I was worried about competition.

I carried my coffee to the edge of the pool and asked if either of them wanted any. Lyric shook his head no. Betsy said she might have one later.

Lyric introduced us. I was Jeannie, the daughter of the woman who owned the pool. I was in Florida on vacation. Before I could stop him, he said, I was taking a break after a fight with my lesbian girlfriend.

I met his gaze and gave him a look that said, among other things, was that necessary? Maybe he wanted her to know that I was no competition.

He shrugged. Then he said, "This is Betsy, a girl who sits next to me in calculus. I told her I'd help her learn to swim. This seemed like a pretty good time and place. I hope you don't mind."

Betsy, standing in the low end of the pool, gave me a shy wave.

Since we told each other our romance stories, I felt I knew a little about her and thought Betsy was pressuring him about more together time, which preceded more touching time. She wore a revealing two-piece swimsuit. Her large round breasts were held in place by a red, tight-fitting top. Her butt beneath the water was round and luscious. I thought but didn't say that she would make a great-looking lesbian.

I set my coffee on the edge of the pool and

situated myself next to it, dangling my feet in the water as I watched them.

They started working with her floating. He held his hands under her. She seemed nervous but slowly pulled her feet up. He let go and pulled his feet up next to her. They floated together for a short time, and then she went under. He grabbed her, and when she came up, she was coughing and spitting. She tried to laugh, but I could see she was scared.

"Why can you do it and I can't?" she demanded.

"You'll get it. Are you tired now?"

She nodded. "Yes, I think so." As she came toward the steps, she asked for that cup of coffee if I still had some.

I checked with Lyric again before I went in. He wanted no coffee. Nothing.

Over my shoulder, I asked, "Cream, sugar?"

"Nothing, thanks."

She won my heart there. If you drink your coffee black, there must be a good spot in you somewhere. I came out with a second cup and passed it to her. By then, she was sitting on the edge of the pool, dangling her feet in the water, watching Lyric swimming his laps. "Do you think I'll ever get it?"

I gave her a winning smile and said, "Many learn much older than you."

"Maybe." Her voice trembled a bit.

I studied her.

She was a pretty girl with long black hair that clung to her neck and back. Her chest rose and fell as she caught her breath. I thought she might cry.

I said, "It'll be all right. You'll get it."

"He's upset with me. I can tell."

He was. I'd never seen Lyric as irritated as he

seemed to be. To him, swimming was easy. I never considered myself a great swimmer. I supposed I could save myself if I weren't in the ocean. Then I had my doubts.

Her hand trembled as she put the coffee cup to her lips.

I touched her shoulder and said, "You'll get it."

She turned toward me. Then she smiled. "Thank you."

I nodded. "Would you like a Pop-Tart or something?"

Thus, Betsy and I became friends. She came into the house to change clothes. I talked to her about school, her baby, Lyric, and the things that her life was centered around. By the second Pop-Tart, I was talking to her about college and her desire to swim.

About once a week, Betsy was in the pool when I woke up. She didn't seem to intrude. And actually, it was nice to have the extra company. I always had coffee and Pop-Tarts ready for her after her lesson.

Chapter Ten

Lyric got another part-time job at a café busing tables and doing dishes through the breakfast rush. He needed the money for college and a car. We went to the boardwalk nightly except for when Mom was home. She worked nights most of the time that summer and slept far into the morning, sometimes afternoon. When he was in town, Charlie got a lot of her time. So when my mother wasn't home, which was often, and Lyric had to work, I started spending the morning and afternoon at the beach where Lyric eventually would join me.

One morning, a man sat on the sea wall looking out toward the ocean. Unless he was watching the waves, which broke several yards out past the tide line, the view wasn't all that interesting. The guy wore ragged jeans and a faded T-shirt. In another world, he could be mistaken for a teenager, but a closer look told me he was somewhere near thirty. He held a lit cigarette between his fingers with a long ash ready to fall. I didn't know if I should interrupt and tell him. If I didn't speak and he remembered me, he might be insulted, but if I went on farther down toward the pier and left him there, he might really need someone to talk to. People who needed to talk to someone were new to me. It came from knowing Mrs. Boyle and my mother, both of whom seemed to need my company now and then. So I sat a few feet from him quietly, at kind of a COVID distance, about six feet away. I didn't want to interrupt or startle him. Time went by, and he didn't move.

Finally, I said, "Pretty day, ain't it?"

Startled, he turned in my direction. "Hi. What are you doing down here so early?" When I saw his full face, he looked familiar.

I shrugged. "Sunshine, I guess. Where I come from, even the nice days aren't this nice."

He crushed his cigarette on the top of the sea wall. "It is a pretty beach, isn't it?"

"Yes."

"You're Lyric's new friend, aren't you?"

"I am?"

"Yeah. You would be Jeannie."

This must happen to celebrities, which I wasn't, people knowing them that they didn't recognize. It never happened to me. So I asked myself where I had met him. Somewhere with Lyric. Most likely Magnolia's."

"Where you from, that sunshine would be so rare?"

"Midwest."

"Yep. That would do it. Where about?"

I noticed then that even this close to the water, there was no wind right then. "Near Chicago."

He nodded, took out another cigarette, and offered me one.

Holding up my palm to stop him, I said, "No thanks. One's too many, and a thousand aren't enough."

He smiled. "Now where'd you hear an old chestnut like that?"

"Back home, I live with my grandma. She's tried to quit several times."

Under the pier, a bunch of gulls found something

of interest. They squawked and carried on. We stared in that direction for a few minutes, yet didn't talk about them. Hungry gulls were part of the scenery this close to the water.

"Where do you know me from?" I asked.

"I've seen you in Magnolia's. I have two jobs. My morning job pays enough for me to work my nighttime job, which doesn't pay as much as I need. Why don't you recognize me?"

"What's your name?"

"I think I'll let you figure that out."

"Oh." I thought our conversation was over, and he didn't want company.

But he told me, "During the day, my name is Rob."

He smiled. The sun must have caught his eyes because he grimaced. "My day job." He pointed out toward the end of the pier. "I work the carousel. It starts in about half an hour."

"Is it busy on weekdays?"

"Not this early. Later, there's a line. I spend a lot of time helping little girls up on the horses. Only trouble is in the evening when kids go out there drunk."

I ran my fingers through my hair. It was still damp. Before the pool that morning, I'd pulled my hair into a ponytail, hoping I wouldn't have to wash it again. But it smelled of chlorine anyway. I scratched at a mosquito bite on my leg. It only bothered me when I was too hot.

He kept talking. "I'll be working at Magnolia's by the time the troublemakers come out on the pier drunk."

"You work at Magnolia's every night?"

"Five nights a week."

He looked toward the pier while I studied him, but I couldn't place him.

He pointed out toward the sea. "Tide's coming in."

"How can you tell?"

"It's the waves coming in like stair steps, one on top of the other." He lifted both legs back over the sea wall. "Here comes your friend."

I turned to see Lyric walking on the sea wall, his arms out to his side to keep his balance.

Rob stood. "Well, it's time I headed out there."

"Nice meeting you," I said as he turned his back to me.

As Lyric approached, he asked, "You know who that is?"

"His name is Rob."

"During the day, he's Rob. At night, he's a dancer at Magnolia's. Could you figure out which one?"

I thought about it. I didn't have an answer. Later, Lyric told me, "He dances by the name of Bobbie Bobbins. The first queen you ever met on your first night there. He was on the stage."

That night, I saw Bobbie's sing and knew right away that with his raggedy male clothes on, Bobbie was Rob, a rather handsome man.

❧ ❧ ❧ ❧

I found Rob now and then in the mornings that I went to the boardwalk. At home, there was Mrs. Boyle, but I'd become very attracted to the water, the sand, and the almost empty boardwalk. Rob and I were both on our own. He didn't talk much about the end of the pier and the merry-go-round, but one morning, he invited me to go out there with him. I was glad to.

We walked slowly. The wind had a fresh sea scent. The water from out on the pier was different than the beach where the waves broke. The sun shone in earnest the first day Rob and I walked to the end of the dock. Its radiance opened like magic.

Rob asked, "You wanna ride?"

"Oh, I couldn't."

"Come on. I'll hop on, too."

We stood before the large circle of horses and wagons. I chose a large black horse with silver reins and stirrups. Rob started the motor and hopped onto an Appaloosa near my side, with only a small white pony between us. His horse was on the inside. The carousel began turning. My horse went up and down. I looked toward Rob, and he smiled. At first, I wasn't really listening to the music. Then I heard it. Rob was playing *Somewhere Over the Rainbow*, and Judy Garland was socking it out.

He must have had a CD player hidden somewhere that played instead of the regular music that followed the horses around.

I said, "Thank you. I love that song."

"I know you do. I got this CD so I could practice. I wanted it just right for you. Well, everybody else, too. This is one of the songs that I don't want to lip sync. I want to get it right."

I flashed Rob a big smile.

He gave me a mock salute.

I stayed out there for half an hour. Then customers came to ride. Rob stopped the motor and changed the music. Two little boys waited by the ticket booth. They were there with what I assumed was their father, probably on a visitation day.

The man passed Rob a big tip and told him to keep the wheel going as long as he felt it was safe. He said, "I'll be over there on the bench with my coffee and newspaper."

Rob pocketed the money and helped the boys onto their choice of horses.

I walked back down the pier, passing a couple fishing. When I stopped on the beach, I could no longer hear the carousel, but I could see it was still moving. The sand between my toes felt foreign.

That night before the show started at Magnolia's, Bobbie confided that after a not very extended ride, both boys got off and vomited.

≈≈≈≈

Lyric didn't work at the café on Thursday mornings. He practiced his laps, working with Betsy, and at last, we walked to my spot at the sea wall and waited until the hamburger shop was starting to serve lunch, which was the same hamburger and onion as dinner. We stopped in and got canned cola, then left and sat and watched the ocean as the tide went out. By then, two middle-aged couples were putting up a net for a game of volleyball. Lyric told me they were there with a cooler of beer every Thursday and Friday. He said they drank and played and were drunk by sundown.

Other times, when I came alone, I watched them play and noticed other people with lawn chairs or blankets beneath umbrellas, watching the game, drinking their own beer. I saw right away that these two couples were good players, although that day, by the time we came back from our walk, they were gone.

Gradually, I noticed more than ever that Lyric was growing handsome. It had to do with the time he spent in the pool, with or without Betsy or me. Since he was working mornings, he usually got up too early for us to swim with him. He'd started wearing a white tank top. Even in the pool, I saw how brown his shoulders were. The tan called attention to his handsome appearance.

It was Monday afternoon, Lyric's only other off day since the café was closed. He and I walked in the back door at 4:30 in the afternoon, just ahead of my mother. He hugged me and left me when he saw her coming. She tossed her purse and keys on the kitchen table and headed for her room. I waited for her to come out, but she didn't. I watched the evening news. By then, I could hear her snoring. I peeked in her bedroom door. She had come home looking old and tired like she used to. She had a wet washcloth on her forehead, which reminded me of when I was a little girl and she came home with a hangover.

Then I heard her raspy voice. "That you, sugar?" She'd started calling me Jean or sugar. I wanted Jeannie. That was all I'd ever been.

"Yeah, it's me."

"I don't feel like eating tonight. Go ahead and order yourself a pizza. There's money in my purse."

"Okay." Frankly, by then, I was getting sick of pizza. It had never been my favorite food. There was a pizza place nearby that also sold spaghetti. I decided to get the salad with it. I was turning toward the kitchen when I heard her say, "Go on and shut my door."

"Okay."

Mom had slept at home that night and had a protein bar and a cup of coffee for her breakfast. She was already gone when I rolled out of bed. She left another note that said, "Drink the milk."

I carried a Pop-Tart to the breakfast table and went back for the milk. The blinds were open, and an empty potato chip bag blew end to end across the patio. The wind was stronger than usual; it made more noise. I wanted to go to the beach later and hoped it wouldn't storm. I had a bite of cinnamon Pop-Tart in my mouth when I picked up the milk and drank a sip.

I was thinking about loss and what Grandma said to me before I booked the flight to Florida. Had my mother caused some sort of injury? Her final escape, she'd left me with a stranger. Did all that followed the years of neglect, my father's death, and my injury make it hard for me to deal with Legs leaving? Whether I was in Florida or at home, losing Legs was terrifying. I hadn't even lost her, and I could barely breathe with anxiety. Loss was always there. I couldn't see any way to avoid it. I finished the last Pop-Tart, and as I chewed the last bite, this sadness washed over me like a weight on my chest that prevented me from moving.

Lyric tapped on the slider and startled me.

"I'm doing my laps. You want to come out?" We'd already made arrangements to walk down to the beach later. I didn't want to get in the water, but it sounded better than sitting there feeling sorry for myself.

"Let me finish my breakfast first."

"Right. I'm going to start." He turned and walked toward the pool.

"Where's Betsy?" I called out.

"Couldn't get a babysitter."

"Why doesn't she bring him?"

Lyric turned toward me. "If she's in the pool, who would watch him?"

I wasn't in the mood for his nonsense. Sometimes I hated the way he talked to Betsy. She worked hard, and he gave her little encouragement. "You know what? Fuck you!"

He stopped at the edge of the pool and turned toward me. "Excuse me?"

I took a deep breath. "I'd rather you broke it off with her than treat her like she doesn't matter."

Hands on his hips, he said, "She does matter. If she's worried about Jacy, she won't be able to concentrate. She's making progress, and I'm proud of her."

He dove into the pool, and I went back into the kitchen and slammed the sliding door shut. For some reason, my anger went away. I dumped out the milk and fried the eggs that Mrs. Boyle sometimes gave me, put them on some toast, and ate them with a big cup of coffee. Then I left the dishes and went out to the pool.

That morning, sad as I felt, we played in the water. Sometimes Lyric threw a soccer ball around and splashed water in my face. I didn't laugh but threw it back, hitting him as hard as I could. He didn't make a fuss about it.

When we finished in the pool, he called me to him. "What's wrong today?"

"I'm sorry. I do think you're hard on Betsy, but this has got more to do with my past than your current."

"Can I help?"

"Don't think so."

He nodded and dropped his arms.

I went inside and sorted the clothes on my

bedroom floor. Before turning on the washing machine, I took a shower. I knew I would, like yesterday, come home from the beach sweaty, dirt-covered, and too tired to do much about it. But at least I'd start out clean.

My hair was still damp when Lyric showed up just after noon. He was carrying a small paper bag.

"That?" I asked.

"Lunch. I made sandwiches. You have something to drink?"

I pointed to the peninsula. "Set it there. Mom has some fabric bags around here somewhere, and there's plenty of bottled water."

Chapter Eleven

This day, the beach had fewer people jostling for a spot in the sun. Lyric wore a flannel shirt, untucked over his T-shirt and cargo shorts. Walking along, at times, I thought he might be too warm. But the sky was growing cloudy, which foreshadowed a rainy afternoon.

I stopped for a moment to catch my breath just past the surf shop and we went on. The sand seemed deeper than before, and each step took more energy. Our surroundings had changed, and the trees behind us gave shade to patches of sand. As we walked on, the air became cooler. Gradually, the shoreline turned into black rocks that rose upward. White water splashed and swirled around their base. I looked back, realizing only then how far we'd come.

The wind sent waves crashing against the shore. Only a few surfers were out.

I said, "Are those guys very good at surfing or are they just stupid?"

Lyric smiled and swallowed, his jaw strong and tan. "I think they know what they're doing. Not many accidents here."

"Sharks?"

"Can't say never. But it's never happened while I've been here." He ducked his head and met my gaze. "You thinking about learning to surf?"

I threw back my head and laughed. "Not much use for it in Chicago."

"When you leave for home this August," Lyric asked, "do you think you'll ever come back?"

I shook my head. How could I explain it?

"Lots of people think Florida is the place to be. Senior citizens and sunshine."

"It is beautiful," I said. "But I don't think I have anyone here. Before now, I counted Mom as someone I could turn to. She doesn't know how to be a parent of any kind. I don't know how I lived through my childhood with her. I pretty much raised myself."

"Sorry. That must be tough. My parents are good people. They just don't like my way of life. I guess they think I have a choice, but just remember, you always have me and Mrs. Boyle here to turn to."

There he was, mentioning diversity again. I asked, "Are you gay?" I'd wanted to ask him before, but suddenly, it just slipped out. Maybe he thought he didn't know me well enough to say so. Although considering all the gay people we were constantly surrounded with, surely he could see I'd be all right with it; in fact, I'd been waiting for him to tell me.

Once again, he shook his head.

I thought that couldn't be the truth. I said, "Back home, I have my grandma. I can hardly wait until I get home to her. She's a lesbian. It makes things so easy. If there were a lesbian facts of life, she told them to me."

His hands shoved deep into his pockets. He listened attentively.

So I went on. "I think most gays go through a period of self-hate and rejection. I didn't have to. Thanks to Grandma, I rolled into lesbianism like you roll off a log." I was sure he was going to let me in on his secret. I asked myself how I could make him comfortable enough to tell me the truth.

A strong wave slapped against the back of my leg, and the sand beneath my feet moved. I jumped and grabbed Lyric's arm.

He caught me and held on. The momentum of the swells was building. "They're probably putting up red flags back near the boardwalk. If you're ever swimming and get caught in a wave like that, swim alongside the shore. You'll never make it back in against the undertow."

"You might have noticed I don't swim well enough to swim in the ocean."

He chuckled. "Ah, we could work on that in the pool."

I looked at the waves. They were stronger than they'd been when we started, and the sky was darker. "I think we're going to get our daily storm."

Lyric pointed toward an expansion of rocks. "There's a bit of a shelter in there that should keep us dry. We could have lunch and wait out this storm."

I slipped and slid in the dry sand.

Lyric seemed to do better. "We need to sit down and try to warm up for a couple of minutes. Your lips are turning blue. Your breathing's hard."

"Sorry, I didn't think it would get this cold. I need to get out of this wind."

The sky was darker. He took my hand and led me into a rock formation.

"Do you know how to get home from here?" Suddenly, I was afraid Tof getting lost.

"Just follow the shoreline. The important thing is to remember which way we came."

Away from the water's edge, a section of the rocks was dark as night inside. Two small flat top rocks were steps away. We sat, our bodies close. My breathing had slowed, but I was still trembling.

"Lean closer," he said.

He pulled my arm around him. His blue flannel shirt was warm against my skin. He said, "Wanna have lunch?"

I'd set the bag down next to me without thinking. I picked it up and reached inside. "We have two peanut butter and jelly sandwiches. Which do you want?"

He smiled. "I'll have the peanut butter."

I passed one to him, then I dug out two bottled waters. They looked good.

I bit into my peanut butter. Don't know why, but it was the best I'd ever eaten.

Another chill caught me. Standing, Lyric shrugged the flannel shirt off his shoulders and put it around mine. I didn't know if I was supposed to put my arms inside, but I automatically did. The flannel wrapped around my body was at once warm. I worked on the buttons. Not far away, the sun was gone, and large drops of rain fell. I felt it rather than saw it. Something had been tight beneath Lyric's flannel shirt. I had gotten used to him swimming in an undershirt. This looked a little like what my dad called a wife beater.

"What's this?"

"A Tomboy chest binder." He raised his arm and showed me a bunch of hooks and eyes. Several were in the last tightest hook.

"Looks uncomfortable." I still didn't understand. I took a deep breath and asked, "Are you injured?"

"It's a binder to keep my breasts flat."

It took me a few minutes to absorb that. I'd heard of men with breasts. Meat Loaf in *Fight Club*, for one. "You have breasts?"

"Most biological females my age have some kind or other. I was born into a female body. I knew from the beginning that it wasn't right. A few years ago, I started changing it. For now, I take hormones. When I'm old enough, I'll have top surgery and no more binders."

The information sank in slowly. I stared off toward the angry sea. The sounds of the waves crashing drowned out everything else. I glanced in his direction; he was watching me. How long had I been thinking? A second of introspection could take a long time.

Finally, he said or rather shouted above the storm, "Is this going to be all right with us? Can we still be friends?"

What could I say? I hadn't had time to think. He'd always seemed like a good person, and if that was what he wanted, I thought I could accept it; in fact, how could I dare refuse him? I smiled and ducked my head into the warmth of his shirt. "You're telling me that you're trans, female to male?" I'd only learned the words recently.

He nodded.

"Of course, we'll still be friends. Why not?" I watched him carefully. I couldn't help thinking that a great canyon yawned between us now. The only cross-dressers I knew were in Magnolia's. Lyric said most of them were drag queens. Trans men like Lyric had been physically born female like me. He kept his girl's body camouflaged, for now. Later, there would be surgery. Tears burned from the inside corner of my eyes. I asked myself what those were about. Crying at that moment seemed stupid and probably rude. But I'd felt sad all day about losses, and I wasn't sure whether I'd just lost something or gained something.

I asked, "How long have you been…you know?" The words sort of stuck in my throat.

"I can't remember a time when I didn't know I was male. I started wearing boy's clothes whenever Mom wasn't around. It was the only time I felt comfortable."

"What am I supposed to do to be your friend?" I asked. "Is there something more you need from me?"

He shrugged. "I've been afraid to tell you because you're the first real friend I've had since I've been living here with my dad. Can we figure something out to stay friends?"

"Of course," I said, although right then I didn't know what, if anything, would need to change.

Lyric said, "This was hard to accept with no one to talk to. I was all alone. I didn't really know it wouldn't change until I hit twelve and thirteen. Then sort of covertly, I started reading and experimenting. I realized my life would be very different from other kids. Once I thought I could just feel this way and say nothing and live like everybody else. I tried. I became so depressed I couldn't get out of bed. I finally understood that this was how it was going to be, no matter what."

I asked, "Who all knows about this?"

"My dad. Mom, of course. She didn't mind when I started dating a girl from the Math Club. In her eyes, I could be a lesbian. But when she found out I was getting testosterone over the internet, she had a lot of trouble accepting it. Next, I got in trouble at school. There was bullying, and finally, one group of boys beat me up every time they found me alone. I begged her not to go and complain. I'd never considered my dad as an option. Then I got a birthday card from him with a nice note in it about a visit over the holidays."

I was way behind in the story. I was stuck on his sexual preference. "Math Club? So you like girls?"

He nodded.

"Girls who like math?"

He shrugged. "Here's the thing, in my mind, we were a straight couple."

"I guess you can get anything from the internet."

He didn't answer for a while but looked at the sand around his feet.

I said, "I'm sorry to pry. This is new to me."

"Surely not all of it."

"Maybe, but we can come back to it later. I know so little." I was thinking I would look on Wikipedia.

Lyric said, "It's all right. I want you to understand. I got testosterone over the internet. It didn't take long for me. My breasts haven't grown since I started, and I only had one period after that. On the other hand, I was soon shaving. I got facial hair that would embarrass a quarterback."

I searched his face and saw no indication of facial hair. Maybe he shaved. My head was spinning. I certainly wanted my friends to accept me when I told them I was lesbian. I now understood that it hadn't been easy for them.

Lyric had his fists clenched under his chin. I touched his arm, and he jumped. His face was red. He stammered, "What?"

"It's going to be all right."

"Really?"

"Sure. We're the same people, aren't we?"

He nodded. "We just know more about each other. When you asked me if I was gay, well, the answer is complicated. I'm a male. I'm attracted to females. That makes me straight."

"How is that possible?"

"Believe me, it is." He looked in my eyes. "I once read that five percent of high schoolers identify as gender diverse. We find each other."

"How about your mother?"

"She knew I was different. I started dressing more masculine at the beginning of my junior year. I saved and stole money and went to the Goodwill to fill out my wardrobe. The other kids hated me, the teachers didn't know what to do with me. About a month into junior year, the bullying started, and then I got a beating. I suffered two of them. Mom was unhappy with me, but the other kids gave me hell, especially over gym class. So I dropped gym and took golf as an elective. But that didn't stop it. I finally told my mother I was going to kill myself or go live with Dad.

"She hadn't talked to him in a long time. She didn't want to call, so I did."

"You told him everything?"

"This was life or death for me. I had to."

"What did he say?"

"He said he didn't approve of it. Didn't know anything about it but to come ahead. We don't get along over a lot of things, but we don't fight about transgender people. One day, I found a book about it next to his recliner. So I know he's trying."

Looking back on that moment, I see how naïve I was and how everything had changed from then on.

I noticed that the ocean had grown quiet. How long had we been sitting there? The sun, low in the sky, reflected in spots on the water's surface like gold.

Lyric stood. "We should go. It's a long way back."

I stood and unbuttoned his shirt, pulled it down

off my shoulders, and passed it to him. "Thanks," I said.

"Welcome. Are you upset with me?"

"Why should I be? I have to admit you've surprised me. But I'm glad you told me. These days, the thing that's on my mind most of the time is Legs and me."

After a moment, he said, "You know, you're free to do what you want or need, like a child running in a field where there are no markings. You can go back to Chicago and Grandma or you can stay here and try to fix your mother or go to Miami and find a way to make up with Legs. I'll help you with whatever you decide."

When he mentioned Legs, my heart almost stopped.

We were late getting home. Mom hadn't come in from work. She'd sent a text that she was having dinner with Charlie and would see me later.

❦❦❦❦

I didn't have supper that night. I called Ruthie and, for once, got through. I asked her how things were going, and she caught me up on some events at the Dairy Queen, school, and the basketball team changes over the summer.

I asked, "How's your love life?"

She said, "Too soon to tell. How about you?"

"I've been abandoned again."

"What?"

"I made a friend the first full day I was here. The boy next door."

"Lyric, right?"

"Yeah. We've been going to the beach together

during the day and a bar at night."

"Sounds fun. Like a real summer vacation."

"Today, he told me he wasn't who I thought he was. Now I feel like the kid I knew has left me. I don't know anything about him anymore."

"Who is he if not who you thought he was?"

"He's a transgender male."

"A girl transitioned into a boy?"

"Right."

"And where does you being left come in?"

I sat at the breakfast table and looked out toward the pool. The sun was going down. Palm trees behind the house were black against the sky. I hadn't turned the lights on, and shadows were shaping inside and out. I didn't want the lights.

Ruthie said, "Are you there?"

I said, "I'm thinking."

"Why do you think he hadn't told you yet?"

"Maybe he was afraid we'd stop doing things together—stop being friends. Every time we went to the bar, I asked him questions about the queens. He didn't like that at first, but he gradually explained things. I honestly thought he was gay."

"So this is a gay bar you've been going to at night?"

"Yeah."

"You are so lucky. I'd love someone to take me to a gay bar."

"I will, when I come home. There's nothing to be afraid of, except we aren't legal drinking age."

Ruthie said, "Okay, back to this sadness. Where did that come from?"

"I feel like I've lost him. I don't even know who he is anymore."

"You know him a helluva lot better than you did yesterday. You're closer."

"Why doesn't it feel that way?"

The line was quiet for a moment, then she said, "It's the way you feel, honey. It isn't real. I've seen you do this before. Legs, for example. Why don't you give it some time?"

"How?" As I said it, I told myself this was nothing like Legs.

"I don't know. But if you let him, I'll bet he can help you. Hell, he probably wants to help you."

I felt a tear slide down my cheek. My nose was running. I walked across the kitchen, got a paper towel, dabbed my cheeks, and blew my nose.

Ruthie said, "Are you crying?"

"No."

"You really are a mess. I wish I was there so I could hug you."

"I don't need to be held."

"What do you need?"

"I need nobody to leave me ever again." It slipped out and felt insane, but it was true.

"Aw, Jeannie." Ruthie's voice had softened.

"Maybe I did lose Legs over this crap."

"You need to come home. This is too hard for you."

"I will be coming home soon. But for now, I'm going to try to suck it up." Probably Mom's lies and screwy behavior had added to this mess. But this was Lyric. He was too important.

"Atta girl."

All at once, we were laughing. Then I was hungry. I said goodbye to Ruthie.

She said, "You gonna be all right?"

"Yes. Thank you."

Before I could hang up, she said, "Keep me posted."

Then she was gone.

Chapter Twelve

Mom tapped on my door and asked if she could come in.

I sat up with my legs crossed and lifted my hair off my neck. "Yeah. I'm awake."

She came in and said, "I'm off work today. You want to go out for breakfast and shop or see a movie?"

"Well…"

"I suppose I can wait until you and Lyric do your laps."

Being so intimate with Lyric yesterday, for some reason, I felt uncomfortable seeing him that morning. I didn't feel like I could look him in the eye. I wasn't sure how I felt about his "big revelation." So I said, "I think I'm getting my period. I'd rather skip laps today." I didn't have to lie to her. I just didn't want to answer any questions about my friendship with Lyric.

Mom came toward me. She smiled as if she felt like a mother for the first time. "Do you need any pads or tampons? I have a few here, but I want you to have your own size."

Well, that embarrassed me. Why should anyone but me know my personal size? If I ever have a daughter, I'll find another way to approach her.

"I'm okay. I was expecting this."

She blushed a little. "I'll make some coffee."

When I came out of the shower, I pulled on jeans and a T-shirt. I wore a bra since we were going out. I went into the kitchen for coffee, heard a splash, and turned to see Lyric in the pool. He was late. Maybe he had waited for me. I called out to him that I wouldn't be out because Mom had changed my plans.

He waved as if he'd heard me. But I wondered…I felt disappointed in myself. I could have done better. At least looked him in the eye.

That afternoon, Mom took me to several places to show me what a beautiful state Florida could be. It seemed to be full of these beautiful gardens. After shopping all morning, we walked through one. I didn't know the names of many of the plants, but I knew Grandma would. We ate lunch at a Waffle House, my choice. Then we shopped at the mall all afternoon, and next, she took me to a bookstore.

She said, "A girl at work told me about this place."

We stood outside the window, and I saw books displayed that were gay and lesbian. She placed a hand on my shoulder and leaned close to my ear. "I want you to know that however you choose to live your life, you have my blessing. It may not seem like it all the time, but you're my daughter, and I love you."

Geez. I took her hand, and we went inside. That meant a lot to me, but it was kind of sappy. I chalked it up to the best she could do and thanked her. I told her I loved her, too. That put a knot in my stomach, and I swallowed back tears.

Books were everywhere, lining the walls and on shelves down the center of the long narrow room. Every kind of book must be there: On a closer look, I found paperback and hardback, mysteries, romances, adventure, memoirs, and nonfiction of all kinds.

At the front end, on a card table that had seen better days, I found a display covered with T-shirts in different sizes and colors that advertised some festival.

A handmade sign above it, about eye level, said, "Lesbian Mysteries," with an arrow that indicated the books were around the corner. One row was against the wall. Above those books were posters of women who were definitely lesbians. I could spend a lot of time studying them, so I thought I should look away. I didn't know how long Mom would stay, and there was something specific I wanted.

I made my way down the lesbian aisle pulling out a book, reading the blurb, and putting it back. Doing the math in my head, I wondered how many we could buy. Then I heard her say to the clerk up front, "My daughter is curious about lesbians. What can you recommend?"

The guy pointed to a special bookcase. "Those are Young Adult books. Does she read mysteries? The ones on this side are popular."

Mom went to the Young and New Adult section, and I went to the mysteries. I could read them and then pass them on to Grandma.

I hurried past the mysteries because there was something else I wanted. Something special. I looked at the books that were turned face out. Unless I knew the name of the author, I was going to be lost. I pulled out a few mysteries, narrowed the ones I held to four, and went to the front of the store, where the clerk was checking out a couple of guys.

The gay couple seemed to be having a hard time keeping their hands off each other. They were both dressed in outfits that showed a lot of skin. Their shorts showed bare legs all the way up. One wore a leather vest with nothing beneath it. He had belts with spikes on his arms and wrists. I tried not to stare. He reminded me of Freddie Mercury, the lead singer of

Queen, one of my father's favorite groups. The other man wore his shorts a little longer than his partner's, but not much, and a tight tank top. When the clerk finished with them, he turned to me and asked, "Are you finding what you need?"

I hesitated. I didn't know how to tell him what I wanted.

The man at the register said, "Honey, you can shop either side of the aisle you want, but the left side of the shelves is for women, and the right side is for men. I won't tell your mother if you get something a little off-color."

I spoke only a little above a whisper. "I'm looking for a book about trans people."

The clerk came around the counter and indicated that I should follow him. In the back of the store was a small lounge. It had a coffeepot and old but comfortable chairs for people to relax and read. At the very back of the store was a set of stairs. As he started down them, he flipped on a light. The basement wasn't anything special. It smelled a little musty. Scattered around were several more book racks, as well as an area all set up for a reading—the chairs in rows facing a small stage with a microphone. I noticed the clerk had a pin on his shirt pocket that read, "Call me Quin." I followed him to a book rack that stood away from the others. And there they were. The shelves weren't as full as the ones upstairs.

He said, "I need to get these up with the other books. I get a lot of customers asking for transgender books these days. There are getting to be so many if you count both fiction and nonfiction. I hate to send people down here. If I put them up there, I'm not sure where they'll go."

I don't know what made me say it, but I gave him a suggestion. "You could move those T-shirts. Put them in the lounge in back and put these on that table."

His face flushed. "That could work. I'll talk to the boss about it. In the meantime, I wanted to come down here with you because some of these books are purely porn. You don't strike me as a girl who wants that."

I nodded.

He pointed to a section on the top row of the display. "Up here, you'll find memoirs and studies. Second shelf some fiction."

"Can you recommend one?"

He reached for one book and then another and handed them to me. "You can sit down over there and look these over. I need to get back upstairs."

I carried the lesbian mysteries and the two books Quin had recommended to the empty chairs that were lined up in front of the stage. It reminded me of the stage in the back of Magnolia's where the queens performed.

I turned *The Pink Unicorn* over in my hands and read the blurbs and reviews on the back and just inside of the book. Then I did the same with *Before I Had the Words*. I noticed that the author, Skylar Kergil, had been putting programs on YouTube. He had a following. I could watch him anywhere.

I put *Unicorn* back on the shelf and held the other book concealed between the lesbian mysteries, so Mom wouldn't see it. At the top of the stairs, I turned off the basement light. When I stepped into the little lounge, Mom was standing there.

She said, "My God. I thought I'd lost you."

"I'm sorry. I should have told you I was going down there. But, according to Quin, the author I was looking for had most of her books in the basement."

"Did you find what you wanted?"

I nodded.

We started walking to the front of the store. When we reached it, an old woman stood at the checkout counter. Her light gray hair hung in a long braid down her back. She wore a faded sundress, the length about six inches above her ankles. The store cat was on the counter purring as the woman stroked its head and ears. Quin entered her purchases into the antiquated cash register. He sacked up her books and gave her the amount.

"Here, take your cat back, so I can dig my money out."

Quin took the animal and set it back on an old blanket that had been folded behind the counter.

The woman picked up her books and gave both of us a winning smile. She turned to go, and at the front door, she stopped at a rack of free papers and picked up a couple of the publications.

After Quin rang our books up, Mom paid. At that point, I did not want to meet her gaze. She might see my deception. Outside, when we got into the car, the scent of sandalwood hung around us like a pleasant cloud.

Mom said, "Where's that smell coming from?"

I sniffed the bag and then one of the books. "It's sandalwood incense. They must keep it burning in there. Probably from the basement."

"It smells nice, doesn't it?"

"It does."

I thought about Legs then. We used to mix sandalwood and patchouli and burn them on the back porch. Grandma never mentioned it. I'm sure she smelled it. We were teenagers. We did what teens did, and a lot more.

❧ ❧ ❧ ❧

After the bookstore, we went to a movie and didn't get home until late. I didn't realize it until later, but I hadn't talked to Lyric all day, and I wasn't sure if I wanted to. I was still trying to push down feelings of loss.

But over the following days, we picked up where we'd been. He made an effort with his lap swimming to get me included. We gradually fell back into our habit. Then one morning, I went out to meet him, and he had a story to tell me.

Lyric stood in the shallow end of the pool telling me that Mrs. Boyle and later Betsy told him about an alligator, a reptile that, despite my early fears, we never saw in this neighborhood.

Just five blocks inland, an alligator had gotten into a family's kitchen while they were gone. When they came home from the store, their dog, who'd been waiting for them at the door, wouldn't stop barking. He ran from the front door to the kitchen doorway over and over. They thought he needed to be walked and assigned one of the kids to do it. The dog didn't cooperate and dragged the kid back inside.

"I think he wants fed, Mom," one kid said.

The woman sighed and went toward the kitchen. The dog went nuts. That was when she saw something move in there. She flipped on the light and found the kitchen table turned over, blocking the living room doorway, and an alligator behind it. The gator had probably turned the table over while trying to get at the dog. The thing was so big it didn't have room to turn around in the galley kitchen and go out the way it came. The Mom called her husband and then ordered everyone else out of the house. The husband Googled, then called the Nuisance Alligator Hotline, who said they'd come, but it took several hours to send an experienced trapper. When he saw the gator, he determined it was so big that he had to phone two more trappers. Finally, they decided they would have to kill the alligator to get him out of the house and haul him away. The trappers weren't happy about that.

The man in charge asked the woman how the alligator could have gotten into the kitchen. She thought it might have followed the dog in the dog door, which was much too small for the reptile, and the sides had been ripped out. The trapper replied, "When it knocked the kitchen table over, it blocked him from the rest of the house. The dog is lucky to be alive."

Eventually, the whole door had to be replaced. The dog door was eliminated. It took a while to train the animal to ask to go in and out. Neither the dog nor the family felt good about the change, but it had to be done.

I asked Lyric if alligators got stuck in houses very often around the area.

He said, "Close to never. There's enough wildlife and domesticated animals to feed on that they rarely come near a human. I've heard they're afraid of people."

The domesticated animals were the part of the story that scared me. It set up a series of alligator nightmares. They always started the same. I was still at my mother's house. Early in the evening, I heard my dog, Diablo, who was really at Grandma's, barking. I followed the sound to the kitchen, then to the sliding glass doors. I saw Diablo round the corner of the house. Then for the first time in my life, not in a zoo, I saw an alligator.

Diablo was running, and the beast was close behind. Then Diablo made a fatal mistake and jumped into the pool. He started splashing toward the center as the gator slid in close behind him. I was paralyzed with fear. I tried calling Diablo, but my voice was practically gone. I thought he might have looked in my direction once, but he was busy paddling. The gator was closing in, fixed on its dinner. I closed my eyes.

I heard a loud crack. Then another and another. I opened my eyes, and the alligator was floating near the center of the pool. It had a few muscle movements, and then it settled down. Mrs. Boyle stood on the edge of the pool with a dripping wet Diablo next to her. Her rifle was fixed on the carcass in case it came to life again, the end of her rifle still smoking. The dream came to me every night. Sometimes Mrs. Boyle killed the creature. Sometimes not. For a while, I cried as I watched the gator speeding toward my dog.

I wanted to go home where alligators didn't eat dogs, where a smart dog could live into old age. This dream haunted me every night until another, more real nightmare came to take its place.

Chapter Thirteen

Pushing the curtains aside, I found the sun rising. I'd heard a noise in the hallway. Someone was outside my door, trying to be quiet and failing. Was it one of Mom's boyfriends? She'd gone to see Charlie last night after dinner. I hadn't expected her to come home until after work this evening.

I tiptoed across my room. All was quiet for a moment, then I heard someone lurch and stumble against the wall. I swallowed my fear and called out, "Mom?"

Nothing.

"Mom, is that you?" That was it. If it wasn't her, then I needed help. I went to find my phone to call 911.

Then she answered. "Yes. It's me, honey. Sorry I woke you. Go back to bed."

"Are you alone?" My voice shook.

"No one here but you and me." After she spoke, she coughed a few times.

I started to go back to bed, but an uneasy feeling stopped me. Crossing my room again, I took hold of the door handle and yanked it open.

She was just past my door, on the way to hers, leaning against the wall for support. She started to slide down, and I grabbed her arm to hold her in place. She reeked of alcohol and was quietly sobbing.

I thought getting her to bed would help. Saddened but not surprised, I asked, "Can you make it to your bed?"

She said, "Yes. You can let go. I'm okay."

She took a wobbly step; I held on. That was the way we got to her bedroom door. She grabbed the handle, and we plunged across the room. I managed to hold on to her, and together, we fell onto her bed, landing with a big *oomph.* I ended up bouncing on top of her.

"I can manage myself, Jeannie. Go back to bed." Her voice was ragged, and she coughed again.

"Are you hurt anywhere?" Before she could answer, I found a lamp on her bedside table, switched it on, and gasped. "What happened?"

"Please go back to bed." Her voice was raspy and harsh. Her face was purple and swollen on one side, and a thin trail of blood was dried below her mouth.

"I'm going to get some ice." It was the only thing I could think of.

"Wait," she said. "Help me to the bathroom."

I wasn't sure how, but I was determined to try. She placed an arm around my neck, and I pulled until she was in a sitting position. Then I put my other arm around her midriff and said, "Help me the best you can. On three."

She nodded.

I said, "One. Two. Three," and pulled upward. I was shocked when it worked. She wasn't steady on her feet, but we started moving slowly toward what I assumed was her bathroom. She was crying.

Again, I asked, "Where are you hurt?"

"All over," she said as she grabbed hold of the sink with one hand, and I tried to help her raise her skirt. She took a shot at her underpants. Black and lacy but backward, they were hard to roll down. I indicated that she needed to hold on to the sink, and I successfully pulled them down. She dropped onto the stool.

I said, "Wait here. I'm going for ice. Do not fall. If you do, I don't think I can help you up."

Panting, she nodded and waved me on my way.

I'd seen it in the movies. A package of frozen peas. Except mine were shoestring-cut french fries. I slapped them on my hip to break them apart as I walked back down the hall. She was standing in the bathroom doorway hanging desperately. I dropped the fries and got hold of her arm again. Then I saw it. Her right arm had a large bruise.

I said, "Kick those panties off your ankles and put your arm around my shoulder." She did, and we managed to stumble toward the bed. She flopped down and drew her legs up.

I found a towel, wrapped the french fries, and placed them on the side of her face.

"Thank you, baby."

"Who did this?"

She started crying again. Snot gathered on her upper lip. I was angry, and I wasn't giving up until she told me. "Charlie did it, right?"

She croaked, "No police."

I said something stupid then. "You two break up?"

She made a strange noise. I looked closer and found that she was laughing.

"Kind of a funny question, huh?" I said, "I'll call the police."

"No. You're a big girl. You know how these things go."

My eyes grew wide. How did these things go? I was happy that she saw me as a "big girl." But if these things didn't end with someone getting arrested, I didn't know how things worked. My mother needed medical attention. If she got it, then someone would be arrested. I didn't think how strange it was taking care of my mother, not at that moment. Not until a long time later, when I told Grandma about it.

I asked quietly, "Do you feel like something might be broken?"

"No police," she repeated.

Someone banged on the front door.

Mom grabbed my wrist so tight it hurt. "Go around the house and make sure all the windows and doors are locked. Especially check the deadbolts."

I swallowed hard. "I shouldn't leave you."

"Go." I could hear Charlie screaming out front. Across the kitchen, I locked the sliding doors, then checked all the windows on the way to the living room. He was screaming, "Let me in, we can talk about this." More pounding.

From across the living room, I could see the door's deadbolt wasn't locked.

It never was.

As soundlessly as I could, I tiptoed toward the door and took hold of the lock. It would snap in place, and he'd know that I did it. I took a deep breath and turned it. It clicked. Charlie pounded on the door again.

"That you, little one?" he said in a creepy voice. Then he made a sound I'll never forget. It was like the sound boys make when they're hunting and enjoying it—about to hurt or kill their prey.

With every bit of courage I had, I hollered, "We called the police. Go ahead and hang around here a little longer."

"I just want to talk to her. I am so sorry."

I didn't respond, and he pounded on the door again. Fear can do horrible things to your thinking. I was so scared I wanted to throw her to the wolves. Rather than let him in, I needed to get away from the door, so I backed up and hurried down the hall.

My diaphragm was rising and falling like a fish washed up on the bank, its mouth open and gasping. I realized I could taste blood in my mouth from biting my tongue.

I walked into Mom's room.

She asked, "He gone?"

"Has this happened before? The neighbors had to hear all that noise. Someone will call the cops. Mrs. Boyle probably has her rifle locked and loaded."

Mom searched my face, then said, "I'm sorry. I never wanted you to see it. This violent side of life. My own mother had guys treat her this way, and I had my share, but I swore to God it would never happen to you." The reference to my maternal grandma did little to impress me.

Ignoring her apology, I said, "Wouldn't it be nice if Mrs. Boyle came up behind him with her gun?"

She ignored me.

"Let's call the paramedics. We can get you looked over and they won't report it." I wasn't sure this was true. It probably wasn't. But if Mom didn't know it, fine with me. One or two more sober grownups involved in this would help.

She held out her arms toward me. "Come here, Jeannie," she said. "We'll wait and see how things look later."

I didn't know what to do, so I crawled into bed next to her, and she put her arms around me, which seemed vile, looking back on it. I wasn't comfortable.

The smell of alcohol was hard to stand, the odor burned like a knife going up my nose. My stress level was high, but my headache, my fear, and my heartbeat gradually slowed down. Then I was asleep.

When I woke, I could hear her in the bathroom again. I was relieved that she had gotten there on her own. Crossing the bedroom, I discovered her bathroom door was unlocked. I called to her that I was going to take a shower.

She was humming. I counted that as a good sign. Maybe her bruises weren't as bad as they'd looked earlier. By the time I was in my room, I could smell cigarettes and booze on everything I wore, in addition to my hair. I undressed and threw the cruddy clothes on a stack that I'd been growing in the corner. She must have left me some hot water because I stood under the shower for a while, washing every part of my body, then I dressed.

Back in my mother's room, I called out to her, "Mom?"

"In here."

Her bathroom mirror was steamed up. I turned on the overhead light. She lay in the bath water squinting at me. I tried to turn my head away.

She sat up and covered herself with a small towel.

I asked, "How can I help?"

She smiled. Her face wouldn't have looked as bad if her lips weren't swollen. "I can't get my arm up enough to wash my hair."

"What should I do?"

"See that small pitcher? I'll sit forward, and you

dump the bathwater over my head."

I remembered that the plastic container was one from the days we'd lived together. Only later did I wonder if she'd taken the damn thing with her when she left Dad and me all those years ago. I told myself I'd ask her, but I never did. Something harsher was coming.

Her thick hair seemed to strain toward me, every root and tendril reeking. I tried not to think about that but took the container of bathwater and dumped it over her head.

She wiped the water from her face and said, "Can you lift my hair off my neck and push it up? It's easier to wash in the tub from that direction."

I realized I'd done the same, standing in the shower, brushing my hair forward, working shampoo to the ends. I figured I learned it from her. How much do we learn in the first ten years of our lives? How much more was there? I lifted her hair again and poured more water over her head and reached for the shampoo. I noticed a shadow on the nape of her neck. A tattoo. There before me, in a lovely script, was my father's name. Beneath it was a heart with an arrow through it.

"How long have you had this?"

"What? Oh, you mean the tattoo? I have lots of them."

"Ones with my father's name?"

"I've had it since before you were born." She turned her face to look at me, and I poured another pitcher of water over her head.

I felt anger rise. "He's my father. He's nothing to you."

"At one time, he was everything to me. I loved

him."

"Don't say that. I don't want to hear it."

"Then let us not speak of the tattoo."

My teeth gritted, and I tried to quit talking, but I couldn't. "You never loved him. You never loved me. While he was in prison, you left me alone for days and brought strange men home. In the end, you left me alone with a man I'd known for less than a day. But I was lucky that time. He just happened to be my father. He was a good man."

She reached for my wrist. I pulled away. I found the bottle of fruit-smelling shampoo and dumped another big clump over her head. She covered her eyes, and I had a tough time rubbing the shampoo in her hair. I almost felt sorry for her. Now I could be the mean one. I could do what I wanted, thanks to Charlie.

"Jeannie, is this the girl you want to be?"

"You hurt me. It's my turn to be angry." I pushed my fingers to her scalp and rubbed briskly.

When she cried out, I realized I'd hit a spot that Charlie had gotten to before me. Setting the pitcher down, I pulled her hair back from her face and passed her a clean washcloth to cover her eyes. After a moment, she said, "We have some things to talk about."

"How could you possibly think so?"

"You were better off with him. He was a good man. I think you know that," she said. "Hand me a dry towel. We'll have some coffee and Pop-Tarts. We can talk."

I let my breath out. The anger was dissipating. "We need to finish this so you won't have shampoo in your hair all day."

"All right, then dump the water over my head and get this damn strawberry stuff out of my hair."

Then she said something I'd never forget, and I'll never know if I understood. "Do you think we all have some kind of compass inside of us, and all we need to do is find it and follow its directions to have a good life?"

I was still trying to figure out what she meant when she went on.

"Some of us start in places farther back than others. My mother was only home once in a while to see if we had any peanut butter, bread, and Ramen noodles—to see if the welfare check had come. I raised my little sisters the best I could. I never knew my dad. I'm not even sure my mother did. When your father went to prison, my mother laughed. She knew I expected my life to change. The only perfect thing he gave me was you."

"You abandoned me," I said hoarsely. "So I wait all these years to get to know you, and you get drunk and come home almost dead. You scared me."

After that, I quietly rinsed her hair with bathwater and then with fresh water from the tap.

❧ ❧ ❧ ❧

We sat at the little breakfast table near the sliding glass doors to the deck and pool. Mom wore a comfortable-looking robe: Soft faded colors were woven together. I was in clean underwear and a sleeveless white and orange Illini T-shirt. Lyric was doing his morning laps while Betsy floated in the shallow end. When he finished, he turned on his back and floated for a while with her, and then she left. Maybe he was waiting for me to come out with a can of soda. Not today. I had this talk I had to have with my mother, although at that moment, I'd lost the anger that would protect me. I just felt sorry for her.

Two boxes of Pop-Tarts and two mugs of coffee sat before us with a bowl of sugar and an almost full half-gallon carton of milk. She still messed up coffee with that stuff. I never would. On our first full day together, Dad broke me in on black coffee. He told me that if I drank coffee, I had to drink it like a grownup. Mom had a box open and two pastries—if you could call them that—lying on a paper plate between us.

I caught her watching Lyric. "He looks healthier than when he first came. Skin browner, muscles sort of firm. I don't think he's gained weight, but he looked pale and skinny when he came to live with his dad. Now he doesn't."

"Were you thinking I'd do that—gain weight and get brown?"

"No. You've always been a beautiful child. I thought I'd lose some weight moving here. But when you have a pool, you rarely use it."

"I was heavy when I was little. Sometimes other kids teased me, wearing the same too-tight clothes every day because they were all I had. One of the things Dad did with his first paycheck was buy me a new pair of jeans. He had me eating right, so I lost some weight and joined the basketball team. I'll never be that neglected child again."

She sighed. "I'm sorry. I hardly know you. I've missed so much of your life." She scratched at a crack in the handle of her cup with a broken nail.

"I didn't ask you to leave that day. Nobody asked you to leave. You hurt both of us."

She squared her shoulders. I'd hit a battleship. A game of Ruthie's I'd never cared for. At length, she said, "I was pregnant."

My jaw dropped. I watched her stir her coffee like nothing had changed. Did I have a little brother or sister somewhere? Maybe she didn't have the baby. She could have aborted it or lost it. Hell, it could be another lie on top of countless others.

Mom asked, "Do you want more to eat? I could cook something."

How could she cook, as beat up as she was? "No thanks." When would this morning end? I wanted to go home. I didn't want to know any of this stuff. And I did not want to feel sorry for her. Maybe she and Dad could have worked things out with another child in the mix. My guess was that Dad hadn't expected celibacy from her. I felt short of breath. I put my head in my hands.

She reached for me.

I pulled away, saying, "If you don't mind, I'd like to go out to the pool to talk to Lyric for a while." Unlike yesterday, his gender change seemed easier to get my head around.

Since Mom had come home ready for a casket, the things she'd said about her life loomed before me. When I was home in the Midwest again, the story she told me and the sights I saw that morning would haunt me. The last thing I wanted to do was talk to her more.

She smiled a hurt smile and nodded. "You go on. I'm going to go back to bed. We'll talk about this later."

One thing I knew, I wanted to go home. I was through with her and Charlie. I wanted my grandma. Without another word, I rose and went out.

Chapter Fourteen

I had to undo the deadbolt from the sliding doors on the way out to the pool area. Lyric, who must have heard me, turned in my direction and waved. I looked for Betsy, but she was gone.

I tried to paste on a smile, but it didn't last long.

I sat, and he pulled himself up on the edge of the pool next to me. Most mornings, we talked while cooling our feet in the water before he put the pool strainer away.

I said nothing until a tear escaped the corner of my eye. I rubbed it away but not quickly enough.

"Rough night, huh?"

I nodded.

"Want to talk about it?"

"No." I meant the tone to be firm, but a catch in my throat gave me away.

He touched my shoulder, and I fell against him.

His arm went around my waist with just the right tension, like a brother or a friend, which of course he was.

I said, "Did you hear things last night?"

He brushed my damp hair off my forehead. "This might be the only time the neighborhood knew something before Mrs. Boyle."

I sniffed and worked at holding in tears. Then I said in a voice that didn't sound like mine. "Charlie beat her up."

Lyric, still holding me, said nothing.

"It's not that I expect my life to always be easy. But I've had my share of-of..." My throat tightened up.

We sat still for a moment. The air was cool for Florida in the summer. Lyric's body felt warm against mine. "I'm angry with her that she got so close to a man who beats up women. Why can't she see who he is? I'd like to use Mrs. Boyle's rifle on him."

"That sounds like a plan." He kicked his feet in the water.

"I know this sounds strange, but I want to take care of her. She's my mother, and it should be the other way around."

He pulled back and said, "I believe you—I want to help her, too. For one thing, Alberta's got to have a good cover story."

"What?"

"Have you seen her car?"

I shook my head. "You mean Mom's car?"

"Come on, let's go take a look at it." He stood and then pulled me up next to him.

I stumbled; his body was warm. His wife beater smelled of chlorine.

Since Lyric came out to me, I wondered if he would want to take the tight thing off. Surely, it would be more comfortable. I was having a hard time thinking of him as male now, anyway. I was pretty sure there was something wrong with that. I didn't bring it up. Not then, anyway.

Later, I suggested he could remove the binder since I wanted him to be comfortable. He said, "It isn't for other people. It's for me and who I am."

The fence to the backyard was a rundown privacy fence with peeling paint and rotten wood. The lock on the gate to the garage and driveway was damaged.

Lyric fiddled with it and popped it open. "If Charlie had been sober, he might have gotten past this gate last night."

I said, "He couldn't have gotten past the sliders. They were deadbolted."

"Unless he busted the windows."

After a moment, I agreed, "Unless he broke the windows."

I followed Lyric around the house. Mom's car had missed the driveway, taken down a small palm tree, one of three that separated Lyric's yard from ours. But the damage didn't stop there. The driver's side mirror hung by a single wire. The front bumper seemed to be suspended in the air. The fender from the driver's side was crinkled and torn partly away.

"Not sure how she got it home," Lyric said.

"Wonder what she hit."

Lyric crept down to the driver's door. "Keys are still in it."

"Should we move it," I asked, "to our own driveway, I mean?"

With a crooked smile, he said, "Up to you. She's your mother."

Then another voice chimed in. "You kids going to try and move it?"

It was Mrs. Boyle.

Lyric said, "What do you think we should do with this mess?"

"For God's sake, get it into the garage before someone reports some nearby property destruction."

I turned to them both as I realized the air was filled with some kind of automotive smell. "Is that smell gas? Or antifreeze?"

Mrs. Boyle came toward me. She touched my

elbow. "How are you, honey? I heard the son of a bitch hollering last night. If it weren't for this car sitting right out in the open and if I hadn't seen her crash it into the ditch earlier, I would have called the cops. I was ready to call them if he got inside."

I laid my hand over hers and thanked her. Then I went past Lyric and tried the driver's side door. It was stuck, but I managed to work it open. I slid beneath the wheel and turned the key. The engine made a strange thumping sound, as it turned over slowly and then caught. There must have been some damage to the exhaust because, in addition to thumping, the motor was loud. I turned to say something and was surprised to find Lyric leaning in the driver's side door, near me.

I said, "I'm going to try and back it into our own drive. Can you guide me?"

He nodded and told Mrs. Boyle to move aside. Stepping to the front end, he got in position to push and guide me.

I put the thing in reverse and started backing up. As I did, something dragged. I just kept going. What could it hurt at this point? The car rose off the palm tree and up an incline toward our driveway.

Lyric tapped on the window. I jumped and hit the brakes. He indicated that I should turn the wheel. I saw I was about to drive into a bigger mess—the garage. By the time we maneuvered it into our driveway, the engine had died.

Lyric opened the door and said, "Get the keys."

We walked around the car and found the front bumper now dragging on the ground. The crinkled fender was pulled away from the tire and lay on the driveway. The passenger front tire that we hadn't been able to see at first was flat.

The three of us stood in awe.

Mrs. Boyle said, "Somebody will call the cops if they see this mess."

Another fear Mom had nailed in my head. No cops. She must have forgotten that she'd wrecked her car.

"Now this is probably illegal," Mrs. Boyle said, "but I think the three of us can push it into the garage."

It seemed impossible, but Lyric raised the garage door and told Mrs. Boyle to manage the steering wheel the best she could. He motioned for me to take the center of the back, and we all pushed. It took several seconds for the car to move, but slowly, it did. When the front end of the car was inside, my heart lurched. We were going to make it. By concealing the evidence, the three of us had just taken part in a crime.

I thought that Mom could tell the folks at work that she'd been in a car accident. The wrecked car would back that up. Hopefully, no one would come knocking at the door with a damage claim. I surprised myself by hiding evidence and coming up with this half-lie car wreck for her. I realized that I was a pretty good liar.

Lyric pointed. "See that mess all over the ground? The radiator must be busted."

Deep tire tracks marked the way from the ditch to the driveway, and a path of mud went into the garage. The car was hidden, at least the best we could.

"Mud is everywhere," I said. "Ground is soft."

Lyric laughed. "Hell, it rains every day. Of course, the ground is soft."

At first, I was angry that he could find this funny, but then I started laughing with him.

I said, "I'm going to get the hose and clean up

those tracks."

Lyric disappeared around the side of the house and returned with a garden hose already spraying. I was surprised that Mom had a hose. But she was leasing the house. Probably the hose belonged to her landlord.

Lyric opened the nozzle and with hard pressure got the hose spraying and moving mud around. The worst of the mud rinsed away with little effort.

Mrs. Boyle put a hand on my shoulder. "You going to be okay?"

I shrugged. What choice did I have? I nodded.

"When all this is cleaned up, why don't you two come over to my place? I have a new chocolate cake."

Lyric heard her over the sound of the water pressure and called out, "You two have it ready in about ten minutes."

❧ ❧ ❧ ❧

Later, sitting around Mrs. Boyle's messy dining room table eating cake, Lyric said, "Jeannie, since you came to Florida, things have gotten pretty exciting."

"Are you blaming me?"

"No. Well, maybe. Life sure was boring without you."

Mrs. Boyle folded her arms across her chest. "Well, I like it. I hate that your mother got beat up. I hate that there was another killing in that alley. But I love that you're here. Lyric and I need more friends."

At length, I said, "I'm sorry, but this is it. I'm going home. I was going to try to make it for two weeks, and here I've done way more than that. Now, I can't leave my mom like she is."

Lyric took hold of my arm. "Please don't leave in

such a hurry. Seems like the only part of Florida you've seen is the bad part. Let me take you to Disney World. Every night, they have a celebration there that's like nothing you've ever seen."

"The things that have happened in the last twelve hours are like nothing I've ever seen nor want to see again. I want my grandma and my dog. No offense, but I hate it here."

Mrs. Boyle said, "You're tired and too full of sugar and chocolate. Things will look better after a long nap and a decent meal."

"Maybe." I'd eaten more sugar than I had since I was ten years old with my mom, waiting for my father to come home. He'd had to fight me, but eventually, I stopped wanting cereal, sweet coffee, and Pop-Tarts. Now after being here for just a little more than a month, my pants felt tighter—especially across the belly.

Then I realized I was still wearing the braless T-shirt and the gym shorts I'd put on after my shower earlier. I'd been so distracted that when I went out to the pool to get away from my mother and talk to Lyric, I had been barely dressed. Women dressed like this in Florida every day. Anyway, neither Lyric nor Mrs. Boyle had mentioned it. I guess they figured I had enough problems.

Lyric stood and started cleaning off the table. The three of us had finished the chocolate cake, each with one or two glasses of milk.

Mrs. Boyle was talking. "If you need any armed backup, you just call, and me and my rifle will be right there. In the meantime, get some rest. You can sack out on my couch if you want. Nobody will bother you."

"I think I better go home and get dressed."

"You two seen the TV today?"

I said I hadn't had time.

"We got us a hurricane headed this way. They claim we'll be in the outer band soon. We've been told to evacuate or seek shelter."

"What will you do?" I asked.

"I'm going to try to get my son to take me to one of those shelters. When my husband was with me, we sat out two of them. Once, the house got flooded in the storm surge, but we made it all right. These days, I don't think I can manage it alone. Won't even try. What are you kids going to do?"

"I'll talk to my mom. I don't know when she'll go back to work, but we'll make a plan. Maybe we'll try to stick it out."

Mrs. Boyle nodded.

She turned to Lyric and said, "What about you?"

He shrugged. "Dunno yet."

"Best have a plan."

Lyric sat and looked in my direction. "You ever been through one before?"

"We don't get hurricanes in the Midwest. I've seen a couple of tornadoes. They're quick, sometimes sneak up on you, and make a helluva mess. How about you?"

"I've been through a couple of mild ones."

"Will this one be mild?"

Mrs. Boyle passed me, went to the living room, and turned on the TV. "Too soon to tell. If it sticks to land, it will probably turn into a tropical storm, but if it goes out across the gulf, it will pick up force over the water. In that case, it may miss us. You have to keep the TV going."

I said, "I don't watch it unless my back is against the wall."

"Better start," she said. "A hurricane is coming this way. And it's everybody's job to keep track of where it is and when it will hit."

I crossed the living room and peered out the window by the sewing machine. "The sky is blue. It looks like good weather to me."

I turned to the window again.

Mrs. Boyle said, "I'll wager the stores down on the boardwalk are nailing plywood across their windows. The surf will be dangerously high, even though the sun is shining. Usually, Ron Don will nail up plywood and then put up the flags, which indicates high waves and strong undertow. No swimmers."

Lyric took my arm. "Come on, let's cool off in the pool. A little exercise will be good for you."

I was exhausted. I needed a nap, but the pool sounded good, so even though he seemed like he was giving me orders, I agreed with him. I thanked Mrs. Boyle and followed Lyric back across the street.

We went around Mom's house, and while Lyric took the stairs at the pool's low end, I went in the house and put on my swimsuit, which was still damp from my last swim. Outside, I went to the deep end and jumped in. It felt good. My head went under, and there was the sound of bubbles, then water clogged my ears. I felt like I'd blocked the world out for just a short time. I didn't care about Mom's car or anything. I did two laps before I pulled myself up on the edge of the pool. The one saving grace of this trip to Florida—the pool. I would miss it back home. I would also miss Lyric, who I later realized had called in sick to his morning job to help me.

After a quick swim, I went inside and turned on the small TV in my room. I'd never used it and was happy when it came in clearly. It was daytime game shows or cartoons. But the local channel had a small square in the corner that showed a map of the Gulf Coast that indicated where the hurricane was making its way toward us. I unpeeled my wet swimsuit and stepped into the shower. Later, a weather girl said they weren't sure which way it was going—to Mississippi or us.

That evening after a nap, Lyric took me to the drugstore to get some Norco that my mom managed to get her doctor to order. She told him, like she told others, including her employer, that it had been a car accident. She'd run off the road, I think there was an alligator in it somewhere. The bottom line was, she couldn't sue someone's insurance, and she didn't have any herself.

Once she had the pills, she settled down considerably. The next day, her boss called and convinced her to come in and work in the kitchen as they were shorthanded. The swelling on her face had gone down. Some of the bruises were starting to fade. If she covered her arms, her appearance wouldn't be so shocking.

When Mom went to work the next day, she said she'd be home at 4:30, and we would decide what we would do about the storm which was coming closer. She seemed sure that it would hit landfall miles south of us and lose some of its steam. Nevertheless, she instructed me to stay close to home. The truth was, she didn't come home that night. I was angry but not surprised.

I'd been so tired that morning of Pop-Tarts and cereal that I found a can of chili and heated it up. Along with that and a stale bag of potato chips,

I had breakfast. I didn't put the heated chili in a bowl but ate out of the small pan I'd cooked it in. It felt like the old days living with Mom. I could have called Grandma, but she would have insisted I come home. Later, I remembered I could have called Mrs. Boyle and wondered why I'd forgotten that. For some reason, I wanted to see Mom through this. Around one o'clock, she called and said she would be home late. It may sound crazy, but my urge to take care of her was as strong as ever.

She still seemed sure that the hurricane would hit the coast and go inland. Again, she said it was too early for hurricanes, and it would probably peter out once it made landfall. At the most, she said, we'd have a big storm. Once more, she told me to stay home.

I decided to get ahold of Lyric and see if he wanted to walk down to Magnolia's when my phone rang. It was on the coffee table in the living room, and I had to run for it. I brushed the newspaper onto the floor, sat, and answered without looking at the caller ID.

Legs said, "Hi. How are things going?"

"Okay," I lied. "And you?"

She went right for my guts. "I've missed you a lot. It hurt for you to be so angry with me. I guess that's settled down some."

Something in my stomach lightened. I said, "I'm sorry." And I meant it. "If I had it to do over, I would have said and done things differently." At that point, I was hoping that I would get a chance to do things over. I'd do whatever she wanted.

"How's your mom?"

"Same. The longer I'm with her, the more I'm like that lonely kid in my deep past."

"Not good then."

She knew about my early years with my mom from the things I'd told her. "Right. Not good."

"I'm sorry. I was hoping you two would connect in some new way."

That lightened my spirits a little. I had someone's sympathy, someone who knew the truth and wished me well.

She hesitated and then, like Grandma, asked, "Have you made any new friends?"

I didn't know what to tell her. Thinking the truth never hurt, I said, "A boy next door. Lyric. We swim in Mom's pool every morning."

"She has a place with a pool? Nice."

"Almost everyone in this neighborhood has one. Mom sublet the house from a guy at work."

"The kid next door, Lyric. Clever name."

"He chose it. It's a long story."

She said it with ease. "Trans?"

"Yeah, it was a while before he told me. What tipped you off?"

"He chose his name. Lucky guess. He must be female to male since he uses masculine pronouns. Are you attracted to him?"

I hesitated. What would change if I were honest? I hedged. "I'm attracted to who he is."

"Not surprised. Most lesbians aren't attracted to trans men, nor they to them."

In my defense, I said, "He's been a good friend. He helps me a lot with Mom. Especially recently. But I'm not attracted to him *that* way. He's only a friend. He's taking me to Disney World sometime soon. After that, I'm heading home." I lay on the couch and put my feet up on its back. "Why do you ask anyway?"

"Just wondered. Sounds like you're having fun. I'm happy for you."

"Honestly, I've been homesick."

Legs said, "Me too."

I hadn't known that. "Oh," I said, asking myself why she was so interested in my attraction to Lyric. Then she hit me with it.

"I've met someone."

Up to that point, I'd thought things were going well with us. My throat closed. My mouth went dry. "W-what?"

"There's a girl here. We've become friends. Normally, the next step would be romance."

I was suddenly angry. Had she been stringing me along? That wasn't like her, if I knew her at all, that is. "You haven't started up with her yet? Do you need my permission?"

She laughed a little. "No. Not permission, exactly. I wanted to tell you. I love you. In a way, I will always love you. But since we've been apart with no future plans, I decided that telling you was part of this process."

"That so?"

"Actually, when I talked to Grandma, she suggested it."

I wanted to hang up on her. Unfortunately, I couldn't manage it. Why were others in my life always seeking counsel from my grandma? I said, "You mean *my* grandma? How often do you talk to her?" I was as jealous about sharing Grandma as I was about Legs's new woman.

I threw the phone across the room.

Chapter Fifteen
(*Hurricane*)

Later, I got dressed in a T-shirt and cutoff jeans and went out to the pool. I sat there with my toes in the water moving them around. I was angry with Legs and angry with Grandma and, more than anything, angry with myself.

I heard Lyric come up behind me. He sat near me but not too near. He said, "Mind if I join you?"

I nodded. "Please do." I wanted his company.

"Now that your nose has completely peeled, you're getting a little suntan. It suits you."

"Thanks." My eyes were watery.

"What's wrong?"

"Legs called me. She's going to start seeing someone else."

The air was heavy. Silence suspended between us. Finally, he said, "I'm sorry."

"I really made a mess of my life. She was the first chance I had to be happy. I made a horrible mistake and blew it."

Lyric took a deep breath and then said, "Someday, you will be beyond this pain. Sometimes you seem to be, and then something like this phone call happens, and you're back to square one."

I don't think I heard or understood what he was saying right then. I kept talking about my past. "When my father died, I thought my life was over. Then I learned to love my grandma, and I found Legs. Where do I go from here?"

He was quiet for a moment, possibly thinking, then he said, "I can see that this hurts, but things will get better."

I pulled my feet out of the water and drew my knees to my chest. Sobs shook my shoulders. What the heck did he know about Legs and me? He hadn't experienced the love we had. "I'm going back inside."

He didn't protest.

As I walked across the patio, I was struck by the strength of the wind. Then I remembered the hurricane. How could I forget something that massive over a call from Legs? Little did I know just what was barreling toward us.

That afternoon, after Lyric had his own house ready, I helped him stack Mom's patio furniture up close to the house. We used the last of the duct tape to shore the larger windows. Then we parted ways.

I watched him cross our backyards.

Later, I opened the curtains. The sun sent a red glow upon the underside of a long rappelling cloud. It hung in the west above the houses, a cry that returned like a chronic bad dream. The palm tree tops that rarely moved were blowing around in the wind, worse than an hour ago. Lightning flashed and then came a clap of thunder.

I made a trip through the house and found my mom wasn't home yet.

❧❧❧❧

When the wind further increased, the storm got scary. I found myself more afraid of being alone than going out in the storm, which was getting worse by the minute. I went looking for Lyric and found him at the bar with several others. Sometime that night, Lyric told me that his dad was stuck at the bar where he worked, which was farther inland and safer. Like my mom, his dad had told him to stay home. He came to Mom's with me. We made our way from Magnolia's to my house and ended up holding each other in the dark hallway as the hurricane raged around us. Now and then, we heard something crash against the house. The front window broke. Glass flew outward. The air pressure seemed to change then. We heard loud crashes from the roof.

Lyric said, "Sounds like you lost some shingles. Rain will start coming in. There will be water, if not from the roof, then the storm surge, which might flood the house from the foundation up. I've seen on TV surges so bad they would take a house off its foundation."

Behind us, patio furniture that we had carefully stacked slammed against the back window; later, I saw that some of the larger pieces had gone into the pool. We looked for days for the rest of the set, finding few pieces. The wind, which seemed to never end, shook the house. Then came a crash so loud that I thought everything was coming down around us.

"Stay here," Lyric said.

"Don't, don't leave me here." I held on to him.

He removed my fingers from his shirt. "We're going to be all right. It can't last much longer. I just want to see if I can figure out what that last noise was." Then he crawled away from me in what was left of the flashlight's glow.

I waited. The sound of the wind wasn't slowing down. I was ready to leave our spot and hunt for Lyric when he returned. He sat next to me and lit a candle. The scent of pine immediately filled the hallway.

Lyric coughed. "The garage came down. A lot has been blown away, but the roof is intact, resting on your mom's car. The sides are easy to see through some big holes."

"I wonder how they're doing down at Magnolia's."

"You have your phone with you?"

I reached for my back pocket, then remembered taking it out because my clothes had been wet. "I don't know where it is. I did have it."

He nodded and stood to go into pine-scented darkness. "Cellphone towers are probably down anyway."

I said, "Think I left mine in the kitchen."

He made to leave again.

I caught him by his still-damp shirttail. "I'm coming with you."

He said, "Don't." But his protest was futile.

We found both phones were on the breakfast table. Lyric's had been ringing at some point. He quickly checked the text, then tried, without success, to return the call.

We took them back to the candlelit hallway and waited. With no power, we were without light, as well as air conditioning. The house grew warm. By dawn, the wind had slowed, although freshwater flooding still came in the form of rain. I tried to imagine, unsuccessfully, what a storm surge was.

I'd nodded off. I wasn't sure how. I was scared. The hurricane was far out of my control, and I thought I might die. Yet I woke after daylight with a single pine candle burned out. I could still hear the wind and drops of rain blowing against the windows that were still in place. The power was out and would be for the rest of the day. It was hard to complain, places close to ours had their power out for days. The only light was gray daylight. When I moved away from Lyric, I woke him.

"What time is it?"

"I don't know. There's a battery-operated clock in the kitchen." I stood, stepped around the corner, and blinked from the light coming through the glass sliders. I said over my shoulder, "Nine thirty."

❧❧❧❧

Gradually, I realized what must have woken me. I felt around for my phone. It was working. My mom was calling.

"Hi, sweetie, you at home? Are you okay?"

"I am."

"I misjudged this storm. I'm so sorry. Are you alone?"

"Lyric is here with me." I couldn't control my anger. My voice rose. "You left me! I've never been through something like this."

She said, "I'm sorry. Hurricanes never come this early in the summer. I thought the storm would make landfall long before here. That would have slowed it down. I guess there's no real way to predict it since climate change."

I braced myself to keep from hanging up. What the hell did she know about global warming? Then I said, "Garage came down. The roof is damaged. Looks like the pool has some of the patio furniture floating in it." For some reason, I wanted to laugh, hysteria maybe.

Mom said, "If there's any place open, I'll pick up

some breakfast on the way home."

That was it. I should have warned her not to drive through standing water. Instead, I hung up. At this point, we had to save batteries.

My mom showed up at about noon. By then, I'd seen a transformer suspended across electric wires out front. When a mess hit the pole, it sizzled. At least she'd had sense enough to find a way around that. None of the stores near us were open, so Lyric and I were sitting at the breakfast table eating from a box of Froot Loops in lukewarm milk. I did wish she had brought some real food with her. When I was a kid, my mom and I rarely had nutritious food in the house. This box of Froot Loops had me revisiting those days: me alone, without food except for cereal, getting up and going to school alone, coming home, hoping she would be there. When she came in, there was no apology. Sometimes in the old days, she brought a bag of groceries. If it weren't for my history, I might have stood her latest behavior. Lyric wasn't too upset; he didn't have my childhood. He was enjoying sugary cereal at noon.

"How are you?" She stressed the "are."

"Fine." I said this in a tone that told her that nothing was fine.

"I see our garage is about gone. The houses on this street are on a little hill. You don't notice it at first because it's everyone around us, too. But when a good storm surge hits, it can miss us. Sometimes it won't, but it looks like we got lucky this time."

Lyric answered. "That garage made a helluva racket when it went. We thought the house was going to Kansas."

I didn't think Mom would get the reference to

The Wizard of Oz, but she did. "I'm sorry. By the time I realized how bad it was, it was too late to come home. I prayed all night that you were okay."

We'd left our phones on the kitchen table. I had no excuse, except my clothes had been wet, and I didn't want to get the phone wet. When I could, I'd made a call to Mrs. Boyle. I'd thought my mother could fend for herself. Our neighbor hadn't answered.

"Have you two been out?"

"Only around here," Lyric said.

After Froot Loops, we went to check on the garage and found Mrs. Boyle standing in the street, staring at her home. She'd already made a stack of trash in her yard. I called out to her, and she turned and waved. I crossed the street and said, "How are you?"

Her arms were folded across her chest. "Basement flooded. Probably lost a bunch of stuff I wanted to save but could live without. How are things on your side of the street?"

"We'll need new patio furniture, although we never used the patio. Probably could live without it. The garage is done for. Most of the fence is gone. We have broken windows, missing roof shingles, and wet carpets."

Mrs. Boyle's voice softened. "I stayed two miles inland and far north of here with my friend Paula. The storm surge was much worse there. Some say it got to six feet. She has five dogs she had to keep safe. We left her trailer and went to the library. The place was crowded. The dogs were scared. We were glad to leave there this morning. She lost a lot. All her goldfish died. Better she wasn't home during the worst of it. She already applied and was turned down by FEMA."

Lyric said, "I'd love to hear the justification they

used to refuse the application for disaster assistance. If this doesn't count as a disaster, what does?"

Mrs. Boyle said, "I couldn't believe my luck when I got home. Not much structural damage. Paula should have come here instead. I'll be all right."

A neighbor I didn't know dragged a bag out of his house and waved.

"Something like this brings folks together. Do you have plenty of garbage bags? I may have overstocked."

Later, I would learn that nobody had too many garbage bags after a hurricane.

Neighbors were already starting to appear. People were dragging items out of their houses and stacking them at the curb. Especially wet carpets.

Lyric asked, "Can we help you with anything?"

Mrs. Boyle shook her head. "I've done this before and will probably do it again. Wet rugs will be too heavy, but I'm far from ready for that. You kids, go help your parents."

As we left, I looked up and down the street, then pulled my phone out of my back pocket. There was a text from Ruthie. In the yard, I unfolded a patio chair and sat to read and try to answer it.

She'd asked if everyone was okay. If Lyric hadn't told me that if the towers were down, we couldn't get a call out, I would have texted her earlier.

I explained that we were all right, but there was some property damage. I asked her to call Grandma and Joyce and pass that information on to them.

Mom was changing her clothes when we came in. She'd eaten the last of the ice cream and set out some hamburger meat that would thaw. Maybe she was planning to cook, but the stove was electric. She'd need some charcoal to cook anything. I'd never seen any at her house.

Lyric said, "Looks like folks are already cleaning up. I got a text from Betsy. Part of their trailer court got hit, but it missed their trailer. Only a couple of injuries."

I had forgotten Betsy. "Should we try to walk over there?"

"If she needs me, I told her to let me know."

Mom, who I'd forgotten was there, said, "Who's Betsy?"

I said it to get even for the way he'd introduced me to her. "One of Lyric's girlfriends from school. Lives in a trailer court behind Walmart."

Lyric shut the slider a little too hard on the way out.

"He sensitive about it?"

I shoved my hands in my pockets while I considered the question. Finally, I decided not to answer it.

Mom said, "You two couldn't get across town. You'd have to walk and at a few points wade. Several streets around us are closed. There's no place anybody can go."

Then something occurred to me. "If your car is out in what is left of the garage, how did you get home?"

"Charlie brought me." I don't think she intended to tell me about Charlie. I was the one who cleaned her up after their last date, but it just slipped out. She covered her mouth as if to keep Charlie's name in there, but it was too late. To hide her error, she said, "I had to walk the last mile, at least, because the roads are blocked with all kinds of rubble. At the end of this block, several trees are across the road."

I met her gaze for a second and then looked away. I was disappointed but not surprised. I wanted to say some useless thing to her like: How bad does this have to get? How many times do you have to come home close to death? How can you forgive him and just go on?

❦ ❦ ❦ ❦

After the squall, people who didn't even know one another worked as one to put things back together. An old lady and her dog were trapped in the ruins of her house. Lyric and I were down there with neighbors from far away, everyone working to free them. The little dog came first, and the workers refused to accept the old lady was dead. They freed her more than an hour later. She had some scrapes on her forehead and a broken arm. Her dog jumped across splintered boards to reach her. He stayed with her and went with her when they put her in a neighbor's car.

Later, we learned that every building down on the boardwalk had some damage, but the only things that were totally gone were on the pier: the far end was missing. A damaged merry-go-round and the bait shop's roof were gone. Our friends at Magnolia's told us that in several miles of coastline, there were marine hazards, large waves, thunderstorm winds, lightning, and waterspouts. Several of those who stayed at the bar told us they'd watched a large yacht float past from the marina almost a mile away. Half sunk, it had been tossed in the water for a long way when it hit the pier and finally went down. The bar lost a front window and roofing. In the angry storm surge, the floor had been waterlogged, and chairs floated around, yet when the water receded, the mud on the floor was manageable. The bar closed until the place was cleaned and repaired. The little hamburger joint fared better than others. It was tucked down between larger buildings that took the brunt of the wind.

Chapter Sixteen

For days, Magnolia's was boarded up. Although it sponsored a party on the beach, followed by a small fireworks display, it missed the weekend business it relied on all summer. Finally, the window was fixed, the floors were scrubbed, and the path from the parking lot to the boardwalk that had been blocked off, the mud too deep, was dry enough to walk on.

In the time I spent at Magnolia's, there were a few lesbians who came in on a regular basis. If any seemed interested in me, I discouraged them. Not that they weren't attractive. I still had hopes for Legs, even after our last conversation, and I didn't want to mess that up with a relationship that couldn't last more than a few weeks.

Lyric and I made plans for Disney World at the end of July. Eventually, I noticed I had started measuring everything before or after Disney. Before Disney and after the storm, I decided I wanted a tattoo and I brought enough money to the boardwalk to get one. I'd made a reservation with Dana in case the shop was busy. But since the storm, business hadn't picked up. The front window was boarded up, and sometimes customers didn't even know he was open, even with signs that said he was. There was little he could do about the window because it had to be ordered. I chose the bird with the treble clef for my shoulder. Lyric would be pleased as it matched his singing bird at the end of his Emily Dickinson poem.

Lyric had the snake tattoo up his back since I met him. It was coiled and raised its head up his neck into his buzzed haircut. He got lots of comments on his snake. More on his new Emily Dickinson I hoped.

I easily got an early appointment with Dana for my own tattoo. Lyric couldn't make the early time but joined me after work on that day. When he came in, I was lying on a narrow cot, and Dana was working on my shoulder. I'd been studying the place to keep my mind off how the buzzing needle felt. I noticed all the little bottles of different colors.

The sun sent beams streaming into the shop through the boards that replaced the windows the storm took out. This day, I saw more than I had when I had come with Lyric. I was mesmerized. The salon was a small room with two chairs, and the scent of patchouli covered the smell of the wet carpet, which would soon be replaced. The walls were still covered with pictures. In the area Dana had set up for body piercings, he also sold jewelry for those pierced. He had three thick books open on the front printing station. In addition, tattoo samples and popular pictures were posted along the walls. I took my time looking at all the designs but nevertheless came back with the musical bird that matched Lyric's. There were two large windows in front of the tattoo stations. Dark now, the sun's radiance could be replaced on an overcast day or at night by adjustable lights above the chairs, so the artists never lacked light. In the back left-hand corner was a table and a rack filled with black T-shirts. The shop's name was printed on the back, and a tattoo design was on the front. Down the center of the room were shelves that not only provided customers some privacy, but also held long colored needles and hundreds of tubes of ink. In the front was a computer that doubled as a printing station and, among other things, made stencils. In this area was the cash register.

Dana was covered with tattoos. As he worked, I remembered his partner, the Russian doll, and it gave me hope that some gay relationships were exclusive. He wasn't a dancer or showgirl like Bobbie. He was with one woman. Lyric told me that many of the guys were coupled up. That gave me hope, as I didn't want to spend my life alone or tricking.

When I asked for the musical bird, Dana had me lie face down on a cot, giving me my first tattoo. The needle stung a little but not too bad. I just closed my eyes. I didn't know why I thought of Legs and the last time we made love. That made me feel sadness rather than pain. I didn't know which was worse.

Dana was easy to talk to, and by the time we were halfway through, he knew my whole history, and I knew a little of his. He was married in a church with his fiancée in a formal bride's dress with a veil. He'd rented a tux, but most of his friends wore formals and sat on the bride's side of the church. People were getting married more and more these days. Dana said, "There's a jeweler west of here that makes a living from wedding rings for gays and lesbians. Since he does that, we go there for any jewelry we want."

"What's your wife's name? I only know her as the girl with cheeks like a Russian doll."

His smile was kind of beautiful. "She hates that, but almost everybody in the bar refers to her as 'Russian Doll' or 'Janis Joplin.' I did that art on her arm. It was how we met. I didn't go to the bar much, still don't. This business was all I had, so I worked a lot of hours.

She came in asking for Janis Joplin. Bartender sent her. Mostly, older folks are stuck on Janis, baby boomers. Hell, Janis died in 1970, before most of the people I know were born. You could say her music lived on for a while. My girl wanted that tattoo, and I couldn't talk her out of it. So I gave her the best one I could. Turned out nice, if I do say so myself. Oh, wife's name, nobody ever uses. It's Dorothy. She chose it after her great-aunt who took her mother in when there was some kind of trouble. Her mother died young, while my wife was just a baby, so Aunt Dorothy raised her, too. This is like a plot from Charles Dickens, isn't it? Except for the gender reassignment surgery and gay boyfriend."

I didn't know what else to say, so I told him how my mother got her name: after a father who left so quickly that she had no memory of him. But she got his name, Alberta—from Albert. It wasn't the same as Dorothy.

By the time I left with my new tattoo, Lyric had come in to admire it.

Joe Smith, the guy I suspected of the killings, came into the tattoo shop as Dana's next customer. He meandered around the room, looking at prints, looking for an image he wanted on the front of his thigh, something big and colorful. He'd be in that chair for a long time and probably have to come again to get certain colors. Dana would be working on him until closing time.

※ ※ ※ ※

Only two nights later, Lyric and I were sitting on the sea wall eating hamburgers and drinking canned root beer. A woman who hung around the tattoo shop stopped and sat next to Lyric. "Have you heard about Dana?"

Lyric turned to face her. "What? Is he okay?"

The girl shook her head, and we waited. At last, she choked out the words, "He's dead. Another body found behind Magnolia's."

Neither of us said anything. The girl hugged Lyric, patted my shoulder, and moved on.

Lyric turned to me and said, "I didn't know there'd been another murder."

There was nothing I could say. I hadn't known, either.

Lyric left me sitting on the sea wall and went into Magnolia's.

I was stunned. Dana had told me he was a husband. I thought that meant no tricking. It seemed to me he would be the last person to be in that alley.

I dropped my hamburger in the sand. As I followed Lyric into the bar, I could hear the gulls behind me fighting for that little food. It was early, and the bar had no customers. Lyric moved toward me, letting me hold him while he cried on my shoulder.

I whispered, "I'm sorry."

"I can't believe these things keep happening. But this is Florida. Probably a gay bashing. Maybe those assholes Lady Ann kicked out of the bar last weekend."

"He wasn't tricking?"

"Dana? Could be, but I don't think it's likely."

Later, most people who didn't know him, due to the police report, believed that Dana had been tricking.

I used the napkin from the bar and dabbed Lyric's cheeks. He took it and blew his nose.

After a moment, I asked, "This guy is a serial killer, a predator, who's treating Magnolia's like a banquet."

Lyric said, "It's happened three times since I've been here. But the other victims were guys who turned tricks. At least, that's what I was told. Dana was married to Russian Doll. I can't believe he would be hooking up with strangers."

"Is there anything we can do?" This was what I'd learned from Grandma. Help out. Take food. Answer the telephone. I sometimes wondered if others thought about who taught them this or that. Probably not. But I'd had such extreme influences.

Lyric said, "Go over to Mrs. Boyle's and help her."

"Mrs. Boyle?"

"He was her son. Didn't you know?"

"Damn it." I left him in the bar and walked around the safe way, down to my mother's house, and then across the street to Mrs. Boyle's house.

The following days ran one into the other. Mostly, I sat with Mrs. Boyle. Others came and went. Sometimes she needed to be alone, and she'd ask me to go. The worst were the phone calls. I finally started taking them for her. Callers understood. Neighbors brought food. When visitors dropped in, I'd set some of it out. The food lasted well past those early days. Lyric carried it all to Magnolia's when an event was organized.

On Saturday night, Magnolia's had a buffet and a dance to raise money for Dana's arrangements. I baked some cookies; Legs taught me this during our first Christmas together. I could think of no better dish. They were popular. I donated fifty dollars from the money Grandma sent me, as money was needed.

Dana was cremated and placed in a beautiful

urn in the corner shadow box in Mrs. Boyle's dining room. There was some discussion of his ashes staying with Russian Doll, but in the end, she admitted that Mrs. Boyle's home was the best for now. A week later, Magnolia's had a memorial for him.

Lyric and I sat with Russian Doll and Mrs. Boyle all afternoon at a table with an extra empty chair for people to stop and talk. Sometimes the line stretched all the way to the front window. From time to time, each of us fired up a cigarette. No one discussed it. Russian Doll just pulled out a pack of cigarettes, opened them, and lit one, then told all of us we were welcome to share as many as we wanted. Lyric picked up the smokes, took one, and passed the pack to Mrs. Boyle, who took one and passed it to me. What the hell? I could quit again tomorrow. I lit my own and laid the pack back in the center of the table. When we finished that pack, Lyric pulled out a fairly new pack of his own, and we smoked them, sometimes one off the end of the other. The extra chair was never empty for long. Magnolia's workers and patrons, at one time or another, had a line of people waiting. When the tattoo shop workers came in, they were pushed to the front because they were trying to keep Dana's shop open. Some people shook their heads, saying we needed to do something about the danger in that alley. One of us would say, "What can be done?" or "Who will do it, if we find something to do?"

From time to time, Russian Doll or Mrs. Boyle cried. I watched Dana's wife. Everyone knew that the men who were killed back in the alley were there for sex. I wondered if this was something that she and Dana agreed on. Or was he cheating? I supposed, in the end, it didn't matter. Certainly, no one mentioned it.

Again, there was a line. In the afternoon, a long folding table with food, both hot and cold, five Crock-Pots, uncounted bags of chips, dips, cheese balls, cookies, and two homemade cakes were set up, and everyone ate. Every time I got up to replenish my plate, several more items had been added. I managed to get the last piece of chocolate pie. When I sat again at the table, I noticed that Russian Doll had two slices.

She said, "Dana's favorite."

I said, "What's not to like?"

I noticed Mrs. Boyle made an effort to include Russian Doll in the conversations. She was the woman's mother-in-law, even though they'd never met. Lyric sat next to Mrs. Boyle, introducing each of the queens. Each seemed genuinely happy to meet her and told her what a splendid person Dana was.

At one point, after a third trip to the table and another cup of strong coffee from a big complicated never-ending pot, I introduced Mrs. Boyle to Bobbie, who sat at the table and bummed a cigarette from the pack in the center and told, as the others had, what a good person Dana was.

Eventually, I ran out of things to say, and I sat there picking at the food on my paper plate. The taste of cigarettes filled my mouth. Chocolate helped a little. Some of the queens I knew better than others. Russian Doll embraced one after the other and cried with each of them.

Chapter Seventeen

After the hurricane, Charlie was at the house often. He did the heavy work, so it was hard to object, but I still did. Especially when he spent the night, which he did all but the first night. He went on the roof and patched, covered still leaky spots with a tarp, and threw tree branches and whatnot from there to the ground. Lyric came to help as soon as the work was done at his house.

While I helped Mrs. Boyle haul out her ruined carpets, at home, Charlie and Mom scrubbed the mud out of the kitchen and took a stab at shampooing our carpets. After the rugs dried, they still smelled horrible. Lyric and I scrubbed, vacuumed, and shampooed the carpet in my room until the shampoo water was growing light. I still got a headache trying to sleep in there. I found a slightly bent chaise lounge, which I didn't think ever belonged to us, and slept on the patio for a few nights with a small oscillating fan blowing in my direction until the rug was hauled out of my room and only a stained plywood floor was left.

The night sounds in Florida, even after the wind blew most insects and small creatures away, were as loud as ever. However, those nights on Mom's patio, I realized I'd grown used to them. I would be going home soon, anyway. Nights on the chaise lounge reminded me of the screened-in porch where I slept all summer back home. Illinois had its hot and humid nights in July and August, but the seasons made them bearable.

Looking back, I don't know how I forgot about the alligators, but I did.

Mom had her name on a waiting list for professional cleaners to come. Again, a reason to tolerate Charlie. His stay wasn't permanent. There were no hotel rooms. Many people were so much worse off than we were. Moreover, I'd be going home soon—I clung to that.

❧ ❧ ❧ ❧

One night, rain fell through the lattice roof of the pergola. I woke to the drops splashing on my face. I pulled the blanket I slept on over my body and dried my face. I fell back to sleep and woke at dawn sweating because I was so warm. I sat up, kicking the blanket off.

To my left were the kitchen sliders. A light was on in there. Charlie, in nothing but his underwear, his belly hanging over the top, was getting a can of beer from the fridge. It was daylight; he must have still been drinking from the night before. I lay back down until he was out of the kitchen. Then I sat up and shrugged off the blanket. I'd been sleeping in my underwear and a sports bra. Both were soaked with perspiration. I walked across the patio toward the pool. Since the hurricane, Lyric had been working to clean it. It looked good. I walked down the steps into the cold water. I saw a couple of bugs on the surface that Lyric would skim off later but no traces of debris. I swam one length and back, then turned over and floated. I must have been in some dream state because a while after daylight Lyric touched me with the pool skimmer. I was startled.

My plan was to go inside and clean up because this was to be our Disney day. But on his way home from the bar that morning, Lyric had hit a tree branch and punctured the radiator. No one in Florida would have a replacement on this short notice, but he'd already found a friend whose car was demolished when a phone pole fell across the rear end during the storm. It had a good radiator. Lyric and his dad were going to switch parts that afternoon for Lyric to use tomorrow. Lyric said, "I didn't think my dad would help me like this. I think he likes you."

"I've never met him."

Lyric shrugged. "I guess we don't argue as much since you've been here. Maybe he sees that I'm happier."

"Look," I said, "I don't have to go to Disney. My grandma sent me a plane ticket for July twenty-ninth. Then I'll be on my way."

"Don't get ahead of me."

"Well, don't the cars have to be the same kind or something to switch parts?"

Lyric sighed. "They do, and they're at least close enough. I'm going to help my dad switch it this afternoon when he wakes up. We won't miss a thing by going tomorrow instead of today."

I smiled weakly. All I wanted to do was go home. Disney World sounded nice—great, in fact—but my proximity to Charlie was getting to me. I didn't want to see him in his underpants, in Mom's kitchen getting a beer. While I could see Mom needed him, I did not.

Lyric put his arm around my shoulders. "I really want you to see this, so you won't go home with a dislike for Florida."

"There are parts of being here I love." I was determined not to cry. "I love the beach and the boardwalk and especially Magnolia's. You've been so kind to me. I won't ever forget you whether we go to Disney World or not."

Lyric held up his first finger. "One more day. Get through today, and we'll be leaving for Orlando in the morning."

I turned to face him. He was smiling at me, hopefully.

I nodded. "We'll go tomorrow."

"Dress light. And it might be better if you bring a change of clothes along. I hope we can go on a couple of water rides because the temperature will be hot enough to saturate you from inside out in the first ten minutes. We'll be in and out of air-conditioned buildings, stores, and places to eat. But it won't be enough. So bring something and leave it in the car for the trip home."

Fortunately, inside, the power was back on, and there was plenty of hot water for a shower. I stood under the spray and lathered my hair twice. From a large wicker basket Mom had gotten me, I put on the last of my clean clothes and gathered the rest from the floor and took them to the washing machine. I'd need them cleaned for tomorrow at Disney and the trip home. By the washing machine, I found a basket of dirty clothes. Charlie's clothes. I opened the lid of the washer, and it was full of wet clothes. He must have had them in his car. He couldn't have worn so much since he'd come here.

That morning, I crossed the road dragging a basket of my dirty laundry behind me. I found myself helping Mrs. Boyle most of the day. Her washer and dryer were two of her appliances that worked. Long after my clothes were done, we napped and watched

TV. We ate a disgraceful supper of peanut butter and strawberry jelly. That night, I slept on Mrs. Boyle's couch. When I called Mom to tell her, she seemed glad. One less thing, I supposed.

Chapter Eighteen
(Disney World)

I told Lyric that I'd go to Disney World with him and planned to leave for home the following day. I made a call to Grandma and got the date of my plane tickets changed, and everything was set. I think my mother was disappointed that I was leaving, but no matter how hard she tried, as long as she was drinking, she couldn't be a mother, even to a big girl like me. I didn't tell her about the phone call from Legs. Lyric was a better shoulder to cry on. I wanted to be with my grandma. I wanted to be at home no matter where Legs was.

The next morning, as I was getting ready to leave for Orlando and checking in with Mrs. Boyle, Mom crossed the street with a paper bag filled with food: two packs of Pop-Tarts, two peanut butter and jelly sandwiches on white bread, and two cans of soda. She'd also thrown in some chocolate candy bars. I didn't think we'd need them, but I thanked her. She said, "Have a good time."

She turned and talked to Mrs. Boyle about the progress of her cleanup for a few minutes, and soon Lyric was in the driveway honking his horn. I pulled the door open to leave, and Mom grabbed me and said, "If there are any problems, you call me. I got your back."

I stiffened and said, "I'll be all right," thinking there wouldn't be a problem or she wouldn't be available, one or the other. Then I wasn't sure why, but I put my arms around her neck and hugged her. She seemed as surprised as I was.

The car was a red and rusty Ford Falcon. Although he'd talked about it, I'd never noticed the Falcon parked in front of Lyric's and said so.

Lyric claimed it was usually parked behind their house when they weren't using it.

The inside was clean. I buckled myself in, Lyric shifted gears, and we backed out of the drive. We didn't run the air conditioner to be gentle with the new, secondhand radiator.

After a while, I got used to the hot wind that blew my hair around. The ball cap Lyric had given me was in my back pocket. I adjusted it on my head, but it didn't help much, so I took the cap off and stopped trying to keep my hair in place. I imagined visiting Florida again one day in the far future and someone saying, "There's that girl with the messy hair. She's here again."

We ate the Pop-Tarts, both packs, with coffee from Starbucks before we'd gone twenty-five miles.

Lyric seemed to know the way but consulted his phone. The trip seemed long. Twice I needed Lyric to pull over so that I might stretch my legs. Both times, I returned to the car with two bottles of cold water and a bag of chips.

Once Lyric had his phone in front of him, he said, "We'll turn off the state route soon, and then it's smooth sailing on I-75 all the way to Orlando."

I'm not sure when we turned onto Interstate 75 because, my stomach full, I'd nodded off. I opened my eyes to some certain yet uncommon clarity. Lyric was giving me a gift. A huge one. As the road stretched out before us, I watched the side of his face as he drove.

I started worrying about money. Lyric insisted on paying for our entrance, which I knew was a lot. The rides were free. After that, he said, our only expense would be food and what we bought in the stores. Grandma had sent me three hundred dollars, and Mrs. Boyle, over my objections, slid fifty dollars into my pocket. My mind went from one thing to the next anxiously.

Driving through Orlando, we saw shirtless kids in small groups playing. They seemed to be everywhere.

We started seeing signs for Disney. We passed huge parking lots. Some were free, and those were full. I think it took about an hour, which seemed impossible, but at last, Lyric pulled into a lot and got one of their last spaces.

"Will we walk from here?" I asked.

Lyric pointed to a tram several aisles away. When we climbed the steps, all the seats were taken, and there was barely any standing room for us, but we managed. By the gates, there were stores with "deal with the heat" products: paper fans, hats, T-shirts, shorts, and tank tops, all with Disney characters. Some folks were buying stuff while in line. Lyric discouraged that because we would have to carry whatever we bought around all day. It would be there when we left for home.

I said, "They have everything."

Lyric said, "People are grabbing mostly bottles of cold water. The prices are impossibly high. Then again, they'll be refillable. But I suppose if they wanted to buy one of the pyramids in Egypt, it'll be in one of these stores."

I had our water bottle emptied and tucked in a

lightweight cloth bag. Its strap hung over my shoulder.

I stayed close to Lyric. There were so many people that I felt a little uneasy. I guess I held on to Lyric's arm a little too tight, and he patted my hand. "There will be crowds and heat all day. Try to relax. I promise you'll get used to it."

"Is it always this bad?"

"It's usually this crowded, and it's always this hot."

He was right about getting used to the heat and the commotion, but adjusting took a couple of hours.

Immediately, we got in line for Splash Mountain. While waiting, I watched logs come out of a cave and fall down the splashing trough. People of all ages screamed, and many seemed surprised that their clothes got wet. The air was hot, and I was ready to be wet. Inside, we stood in line in the darkness, and the crowd around us disappeared, and out of the blue, total strangers were talking to one another.

When our log was at the top of the channel, I screamed, although I knew what was coming. I screamed all the way down. It was wonderful.

We waited for a second water ride with a long waiting line. My body had quickly dried off after what Lyric called the log ride. Again, the line was a long wait, and again, in the end, it was worth it.

My hair was plastered to my forehead. Lyric's ball cap was in my back pocket again. I thought it was making my head hot. We stood in a much shorter line to get some lunch. Eventually, we got chairs and caught our breath for a while. I felt exhausted. I had been ignoring it, and I was determined to do so as long as Lyric could.

After lunch, we stood in a little shorter line for

attractions like the Haunted Mansion, my choice, and It's a Small World—how could we ignore it with that song that seemed to be everywhere? And another water ride before we headed for a good spot to see the fireworks. We sat on the edge of a fountain. Lyric warned me that we were going to stand when the show started because people would crowd in front of us.

The fireworks were amazing and seemed to go on forever. Every few seconds, the crowd carried on about a new and better bomb. The impressions of several spidering lights against the dark sky and behind Cinderella Castle were breathtaking.

Then in the middle of everything, someone tapped on my shoulder. I didn't turn at first because I was with the only other person I knew at Disney World. My shoulder was tapped again, this time a little harder. I turned, and there I was face-to-face with one of the seven dwarfs, Grumpy. The dressed-up characters hadn't paid any attention to the adult-sized me until then. Lyric laughed, held up his phone, and got a few pictures. Before we left, I bought a Grumpy T-shirt that I carried home and, in the fall, wore to school at least once a week. When I wore it, I remembered that night, the most beautiful fireworks I'd ever seen, and the Disney character who came to me. While I was standing there in an unbelievably close crowd, something flew over my head. I sort of ducked. The children around me were excited. A little girl next to me had convinced her father to hold her on his shoulders.

I called out to her, "What is that thing?"

She shouted, "Tinkerbell."

The animated image gave quite a show while excited children screamed.

After the fireworks, we headed home. It was very late, but that didn't preclude a traffic jam. Parents with weary children were packing it in.

As Lyric carefully inched through the traffic, I closed my eyes and relived the explosions of light behind the castle—the most beautiful thing.

I knew then I would never forget this day, and I said so to Lyric. He smiled and told me he was glad. He swung the car onto the road, and then we were working ourselves into a long line of cars. He reached across the front seat and touched my arm. "I'm going to miss you."

"And I you."

The night was cooler. With the open windows, the car was almost too cool. Several miles down the road, as we turned onto the state route, I noticed steam coming out from under the hood.

At the same time, Lyric said, "Uh-oh." A red light on the dash came on. He slowed the car and pulled off the road.

"What is it?" I asked.

"We've overheated."

"The radiator?"

"'Fraid so."

With the car stopped, he got out, went to the front end, and raised the hood. I got out and watched him. The radiator was boiling, throwing steam in all directions.

Lyric said, "She's got another leak."

With my hands in my pockets next to him, I watched the steam.

He said, "I hate to, but I'm going to call my father."

"I'm sorry."

"It's not your fault." He took his phone out and walked several feet ahead of me. He talked for a moment and then looked around. When he hung up, he came to me and said, "See that gas station just off the next exit?"

"Yeah." It was small, and the lights were off.

"Dad said to push the car down off the road and just stay in it until he can get here tomorrow afternoon."

"What can he do tomorrow?" I was starting to think I'd never get out of Florida. I wanted to be on the flight home tomorrow. I wanted to see my grandma and my dog. I couldn't say those childish things. Lyric had enough on his mind without me falling apart.

"He has to borrow a truck from his boss, rent a tow bar, and come get us."

"Well, at least we aren't stranded here."

"Look. I'm sorry," he said. After a moment, he followed with, "I wanted this to be a special night for you to remember me by."

I said, "This is an adventure I won't forget."

"I didn't mean in your nightmares."

"Nor did I."

He looked me in the eyes for a moment and then said, "Let's start by getting this car rolling."

With the front door open, he directed me to the driver's side. "When we get her rolling, jump in and start steering. Take that exit and go down the hill, do not put the brakes on unless you have to. Pull into the little gas station down there. Get her out of the way as best you can."

All the lights were out, and the station was closed. I didn't think we could get the car to roll, but gradually, it did. After a few feet, I heard Lyric call out, "Get in."

I told myself this could be dangerous, but I jumped in anyway and reached to close the door; it swung shut on my leg. Pushing the door back, I pulled my leg inside, and the door closed. I'd probably have a bruise down there for a while. The steering wheel was tight. Difficult to turn. But soon we were going fast enough that I thought I might not make the downhill turn. Throwing gravel, I drove on the dark exit ramp. All I could see was in my headlights. About halfway down the ramp, I saw it—a little two-pump station with walls of chipped white paint. Lyric jumped in the passenger door. "Pull around to the side and hit the brakes. Sometimes, automatic brakes with the engine off can be hard to work, so hit them hard." I did as he said, and then I saw the land drop away down a steep hill just beyond the building. I hit the brakes with everything I had. The car stopped.

I set the emergency brake, opened the door, and got out. I had no idea where I was going. I bent and looked inside the car and saw Lyric with his head in his hands. "You all right?" I asked.

He nodded and reached for the passenger door handle.

I was startled by a voice behind me. "What are you kids doing?"

I turned to see an old man leaning against the building, with white whiskers and his thumbs hooked in the straps of his overalls.

Lyric said, "We had some car trouble up on the highway. We can't get help until tomorrow afternoon. I hope it's all right if we park here."

"Well, I don't reckon the boss would mind. Y'all gonna sleep here?"

I said, "We don't have anywhere else."

The old man scratched his chin and then said, "Boss owns that little motor court just up the way. Since you have so much time to wait, you could get an air-conditioned room and a TV to pass the time. Boss would take it a lot easier if you was a paying customer."

My gaze followed his finger, and I could see a flashing red light far away that might have said, "Vacancy."

I glanced across the top of the car at Lyric. He shrugged. "If you want, it beats sleeping all night and spending half of tomorrow in this hot car."

We thanked the old man whose name we never did get, gathered our things, locked the car, and started walking toward the motel.

The old man followed us up the road and hurried across the parking area to open the motel office. Inside, he was all business. He got out a register and turned it toward us. He took our money and assigned us the room, front on the far end. Before we left the office, we were directed to the passageway that contained a Coke machine and a vending machine full of gum, chips, nuts, and candy standing against one wall. We loaded up. I personally preferred peanut butter crackers. I emptied the machine of those, laid our booty in the tops of our bags, and then made the trip down the walk to the room we were assigned. None of the other rooms appeared rented. I didn't care. I was looking forward to a bed and air conditioner for the night.

Inside, Lyric turned to me and said, "Don't get me wrong, I'm glad to have found this place, but what do you think the deal is with that old guy?"

I shrugged. "Kind of Alfred Hitchcock. You know *Psycho*?"

He smiled. "We'll each have to watch as the other showers."

And that was how our pivotal night began—with laughter.

Chapter Nineteen
(*Things change*)

I felt exhausted. My skin was sticky from the constant sweating and still warm from a new sunburn. I tossed my bag on the bed nearest the door and looked around. The room was small and shabby. It smelled of cigarette smoke and ancient dust. The air was warm but not as bad as the day had been.

Lyric shut and locked the door behind him and went directly to the window air conditioner. He messed with it for a moment, and then it was running to suit him, albeit noisy. He went to the bed that I hadn't staked out, stacked the two pillows, and fell across the bedspread. "You see the remote?"

I did not. In fact, I was pretty sure we didn't have one. "Maybe this is one you have to use the knobs to turn on and change channels."

Lyric groaned, stood again, and approached the TV. Soon it flickered on, and he found a station that was tolerable. Lying back across the bed, he said, "You smell cigarette smoke?"

"I do, but I wasn't going to mention it. I smoked way too much this summer. I've quit, remember?"

"So as a quitter, it doesn't bother you as much?"

"It bothers me more."

"When did you start? How old were you?"

"Don't remember. I had a good addiction going by the time my mother left when I was ten. Then I stole cigarettes from Grandma."

Switching topics, Lyric said, "If you want to take the first shower, go ahead. I can wait."

I sat on the edge of my bed and gathered my clean clothes. Then I stood and went through a small white door to the bathroom. It was a simple little room: a toilet, sink, a bathtub that doubled as a shower. I found a small wrapped-up soap and a tiny bottle of shampoo. The washcloth and towel were clean but scratchy. I turned on the water in the tub. It came out cold. That worried me a little, but the water gradually warmed up. I dropped the clothes I'd worn on the floor and kicked them to the corner. I unwrapped the soap and put the shampoo on the edge of the tub.

The water pressure wasn't great, but it felt good. I soaped up and rinsed. It took the entire bottle of shampoo to lather my head. Luckily, Lyric didn't have more than a quarter of an inch of hair, and he could manage without shampoo. Not wanting to use all the hot water, I hurried to rinse off.

After the shower, I wrapped myself in the largest white towel, returned to the main room, and sat on the end of my bed. I was nice and clean, and fatigue set in. The TV was on a fifties Western. I watched, but my eyes were drooping. I tried to wrestle a small comb I'd wrapped in my clothes through my wet hair. It was tangled, but I did the best I could. Sitting on the bed, the towel around me, I pulled on my fresh clothes and crawled beneath my single sheet and closed my eyes.

I dreamed of fireworks beneath the torrid Florida sky, over a beautiful castle with Tinkerbell, ducking and soaring, flying over my head, among hundreds of children all up past their bedtimes, screaming with joy. For the rest of my life, I could say I'd been to Disney World. That would mean more back in Illinois. Then seemingly from nowhere, Grumpy found me and tapped on my shoulder. I took it as a sign.

Lyric was asleep in the clothes he'd worn all day.

He woke me when he raised his right arm from beneath his head and rolled on his side. A moment later, he was on his feet. I watched him go into the bathroom. Out of the corner of my eye, I saw him drop his clothes. His legs and arms were brown from the sun. His hips spread a little. His shoulders were square—maybe from swimming laps in Mom's pool. He hadn't closed the door. I'd wondered what his body looked like, and there he stood, looking at me. Steam rolled from the shower. I realized I was seeing all of him in a mirror on the back of the bathroom door, from which, if he wanted to, he could have watched me as I showered. I turned, looked at the TV, and did not look at the bathroom again until Lyric was out and had his extra outfit on.

"You awake?" he asked.

I rolled over.

"You hungry?"

"I could eat, but I've finished my crackers, and from where we are, a meal is impossible."

"I saw a pizza place at the last exit."

"That was at least twenty miles back. And they're probably closed this late."

"Farther than twenty, I think. But we could take a crack at getting them to send one. We might have to add money for a long delivery. Let's try it." He seemed excited. "My dad said he'd be here tomorrow. But he's going to have to borrow a truck and rent a tow bar. We won't be headed home until the afternoon. Might as well try to get something to eat."

Lyric used his phone to Google a pizza place.

There was only one. He asked me what I liked on pizza. There was always trouble with me because I wanted only sausage and cheese. Sometimes only cheese. But when I told him, he behaved like it was the most normal thing in the world. He called the place and gave them our order, half my way and half his, then he had a tense discussion about us being so far away. Finally, it was settled. He'd give them an extra twenty dollars above the order and the tip. It took over an hour for the delivery guy to find us. We had both nodded off when a knock came at the door. Lyric jumped up and, without asking who was there, swung the door open.

He paid, and we were opening the box on Lyric's bed. We ate until we were stuffed. The pizza box and the few remains were put on Lyric's bedside table.

❦❦❦❦

We were both awake before dawn. Lyric went to see if there was coffee in the office. It was closed. He got us Cokes and came back to the room.

Then everything between Lyric and I changed. You might say both our lives changed.

We drank Cokes and ate what pizza slices were left over.

I said, "Even with this night, I've enjoyed Disney World and everything since then. I don't know what this visit with my mother would have been like without you. I'll miss you."

He shyly said, "Thanks."

"I've never known anyone like you."

He looked at the floor and then said softly, "I'm not as unusual as you might think." Then seemingly out of nowhere, he added, "Would you let me touch you?"

I hesitated. I'd naïvely thought that sex wasn't possible for us. I was a lesbian, and he was a man. He'd told me that he wanted a woman who wanted a man. I hadn't thought of being with anyone but Legs, ever. The plan for my life centered on finding her and making up. But I loved Lyric. I would always love him. That didn't mean we had to have sex. It also didn't mean we wouldn't. My mind jumped from one thing to the next. I thought about his girlfriend in the Math Club. Had they been intimate? I asked myself if there would come a day when Betsy would have hard feelings about him touching me. Plus, how could I be with Lyric and then go back to Legs? I knew one thing; I would have to tell her.

I said, "When I go home, I'll try to make up with Legs. I don't see it as fair to start up with you and then run after her."

Lyric said, "I thought as much. But after you leave, we probably won't see each other. I can't imagine you coming back to visit your mother again. Could you cope with just this one time?"

He got up and moved to the end of my bed wearing only his new Badassed Mickey T-shirt, which made him look hot. I didn't have words to answer his question. Actually, I didn't know. On the surface, it sounded simple. I hesitated and asked myself what it would be like to be touched by Lyric. I found myself wanting him.

Looking back, I could see that nothing was settled before he walked around the end of the bed, took my face in his hands, and covered my lips with a kiss that I couldn't help but return. He ran his hands down my arms, then he stopped. He pulled my T-shirt over my head. I helped him unfasten my jeans, push them down, and kick them off my feet. He lay in the bed next to me. His body was warm against mine, his stomach and chest pressed against my frame. My nerve ends tingled, and I told myself there would be a price for this, but at that moment, I didn't care.

He got up on his knees and pinned me to the bed. I balled my hands into the sheet to steady myself. My next move was to fling him away. He studied my naked body while my own arousal blossomed. I stammered, "What should I do? What gives you pleasure?"

I wasn't sure he heard me. He was studying my breasts. The nipples were erect and hard. He squeezed them softly, bent his head, and took one nipple in his mouth, sucking the small pink bud to rock hardness. He then swirled his tongue around and dragged his lips over the swell of my breast. He moved to the second one and repeated the same. Both nipples were wet and rigid. I asked again, "What gives you pleasure?"

He raised his head and looked me in the eyes. "I'm enjoying this. Aren't you?"

"Of course," I said. "But I'm a little confused by my attraction to you and yours to me. I'm a lesbian, and you're...you're..."

He smiled and kissed my forehead. "I don't want to explain this in the middle of sex, but you seem to need me to. Probably anyone can be attracted to anyone. Myself, I prefer women—straight women. But over the last several weeks and all day today, I've fallen in love with you, and I want to make love to you. So how about you tell me what pleases you and I'll do my best?"

"You've fallen in love with me?"

His voice grew soft. "Yes. I didn't mean to tell you because I totally understand your love for Legs and your desire to return to your life with her. So I've had desires I haven't acted on. But tonight, I want to know what pleases you."

My head was spinning. I agreed this was a conversation we should have had before we were lying in bed together. "Please, go on."

His hands traced the sides of my body. His face was still near mine and instead of a kiss, he bit my lip, then kissed his way downward. With each kiss, he gave a little more pressure. The constant changing of his pressure left me a wreck. When he came to the spot between my legs, two fingers stroked my outer lips. I spread my legs. I was as wet as I ever had been. I knew his lips would touch me there. I'd done this often with Legs, and I loved it.

I gave his head a little push.

He looked up at me, smiling. "Be patient. I want this to last all morning." He pushed his fingers into my folds, penetrated me, and rubbed my clit with his thumb. Then he thrust inside me even farther, pulled me open, and licked me, burying his face in me. I couldn't help moving my hips in a grinding motion.

His tongue seemed to be everywhere, leaving moist trails of heat. He pumped his fingers in and out and up and down until I felt like I might explode. Then with a choking cry, I came.

Later, I told myself that I could have stopped anytime. I could have said no. But I wanted him. Sometimes there comes to each of us an event, something you know you shouldn't do, but you can't *not* do it. I had different plans for my life, and there would be consequences for this, but I was swept up in it.

For me, Legs was gone. My plans were gone. There was only Lyric and me rolling around on that motel bed.

He climbed up beside me, and we caught our breath for a moment. I was ready to reciprocate. I ran my hand down his belly, and he stopped me. "Did you ever hear of tribadism?"

"Rubbing together?"

"Yes."

I'd done it once or twice with Legs when I had my period. "That would please you?"

"Yes. Bend your leg."

He ran his hand through my wetness and spread it on my thigh. Then he lay on top of me and wedged my thigh under his leg.

He whispered, "I like this because we face each other."

At least, I think that was what he said. His whisper was extremely soft and gentle.

When he was in an ideal position, his body moved against mine. Not knowing what to do, I let him move backward and forward until my leg was touching his. He increased his strokes, then a sound escaped his throat, and his body stiffened as he came.

I rolled on top of him, hungrily devouring his salty neck. Each breath was coming quickly. I ran my hand down his body, but he gently pushed it away.

"No?" I asked.

He gave me a long, wet kiss, then said, "No. Sometimes, but not now. I'm satisfied."

We lay entwined on top of the sheets breathing hard for a while.

I said, "I need to ask you a question."

"If it's about getting married, I think we're too young." He laughed.

"No," I said. "I didn't think you had much experience."

"Well, I'm an avid reader. The girl in the Math Club taught me a lot. There have been others. Some straight women."

"What you did was like the things I do with Legs. For me, the experience wasn't new, but the partner was, and that changed everything."

He said, "I suppose it gets complicated to someone who's never had a trans lover."

"But you were satisfied?" I asked.

"Yes. Tremendously. Can we leave it at that?"

I turned over on my side, and he spooned behind me. As I closed my eyes, I said one last thing. "Lyric, I love you, too."

He squeezed me.

Then my grandma's voice was in my head saying, like always, "You've said enough. Let sleeping dogs lie."

So we drifted off to sleep.

❧❧❧❧

We woke to Lyric's phone ringing.

"Hi, Dad."

Then he said, "Car's just off the exit just after you turn onto the state route. We pushed it off the main road and found a little gas station to park it."

They said a few more things that I didn't hear because I was busy gathering my clothes and putting them on as if his dad could see me.

Lyric hung up and turned to me. "He's about an hour away. We have time for more lovemaking."

"I just want to get dressed and wait. Suppose he's early."

Lyric accepted that, even though he knew it was our last time ever. He reached for his shorts and pulled them on. "Whatever you say, Jeannie. Whatever you say."

He went into the bathroom and finished dressing.

Lyric's dad found us without much trouble. When Lyric introduced us, his dad asked if I had a good time at Disney World. I told him it was wonderful. The two of them hooked the tow bar to the truck and then the Falcon to the tow bar, while I stood watching them. I asked if I could help, and they exchanged a smile that let me know they thought the idea was ludicrous. We got into the truck, me in the middle, Lyric on the passenger side, and his dad driving. I tried to be as small as I could, but I was aware of Lyric's thigh pressing on mine all the way home.

I would think about that day for a long time. Something preyed on my mind. There was no one to ask, not even Lyric. I wondered if sexuality came from the body or the brain. Logic didn't help me with that. I might ask Grandma when I got home. I remembered my analogy about the shades of gray. If straight was white and gay was black, I always considered myself a charcoal gray. Had that changed? Of course, it had! I just wasn't sure where the needle had landed. Accepting lesbianism had been easy, and maybe that was what I still was. But figuring out the uncounted options was more difficult. I couldn't even say what I wanted to be.

When the truck prepared to back into Lyric's driveway, he got out to guide his dad. I jumped out behind him and waved goodbye to both of them. I was almost to my mother's door when Lyric put a hand on my shoulder and spun me around. He hugged me.

Chapter Twenty

When I came through the backdoor, I found Charlie stretched out in the living room with a beer and a cigarette. Mom, he said, was working the day shift. He didn't get up but asked, "Have a nice time?"

I said, "Yes," attempting to head for my bedroom.

"I heard you had car trouble. Everything okay?"

How would he know that? I didn't want to talk to him and didn't want to be alone in the house with him. I said, "I'm fine. Car needs a radiator."

"Sorry to hear that." He took a drag off his cigarette and went on, "How'd you like Disney?" This was more words than he'd ever said to me.

Trying to escape, I almost had my back to him, but I stopped and turned. "It was great. Thanks for asking."

"Well, at least now you know that Florida has more to offer than heat and hurricanes."

I almost convinced myself that he wasn't who he was, and he was just making small talk. So I yawned, trying to avoid making a big deal out of it. "After the day I've had with the car breakdown, I'm exhausted. I'm going to lie down for a while."

He took a long swig of beer. "Oh, don't let me keep you. If you're hungry, there's some cold pizza left from our dinner last night and Pop-Tarts. Alberta has started keeping those things around."

"Thanks. Maybe later. I just want a nap right

now." After pizza late last night and bits of crust for breakfast, the thought of pizza nauseated me. I was a little hungry, but I decided to wait until Mom was home to eat.

When I got into my bedroom, I checked to see if there was a lock on the door. In all the times I'd been there, I'd never looked. It turned out that Mom's room had one, but mine did not. I didn't like Charlie, but he really hadn't done anything to scare me except be his exasperating self—that and nearly murder my mom. I didn't undress but lay on the bed and stared at the ceiling until I dozed off.

My phone woke me. I found it in my back pocket with the black cap, my first gift from Lyric.

"Jeannie?" Grandma's voice.

"It's me. I'm so glad to hear from you. Mom exchanged my ticket for early tomorrow morning. I should be at O'Hare by noon." Without me to remind her, I worried about Mom remembering to change my flight and tell Grandma. I wanted the earliest flight possible.

"We'll all be glad to have you home. Especially Diablo. He just wanders around the house like he's lost without you."

"I miss him, too. I miss everyone."

"You've been to Disney World with your friend. It was yesterday, wasn't it?" Grandma asked.

"Yes. It was great, but we had some car trouble on the way home. We had to wait for Lyric's dad to come and tow us. We didn't get back here until this afternoon. The first thing, I took a nap."

"Did I wake you?"

"Don't worry about it. I have things I want to do before I pack. I've been crossing the street to Mrs.

Boyle's, spending time there. Her son was murdered. I lost a father the same way. I don't know if I helped her, but she's a friend, and I can just be with her."

Grandma said, "I'm so sorry. You're a good girl to try to help her."

"Thanks. I feel so powerless."

"What about that boy next door? Are we going to hear any more about him?"

I yawned and searched for the right thing to say. I couldn't tell her that I slept with him, that I loved him, he loved me, and I was never going to see him again. It sounded outrageous. No eighteen-year-old girl could tell her grandma something like that. I chose my words carefully. "We've grown to be good friends. I'll miss him, but I can't imagine how we'll ever see each other again."

"Honey, that sounds overly dramatic. Life is full of twists and turns."

"Stop that, you're scaring me."

We both laughed. She a little longer than I did.

Then I said earnestly, "I don't think I'll ever come back to Florida."

"So how *is* your mother?"

I paused and then said, "We get along fine. Since the storm, Charlie has been here a lot. He's helping with repairs. But he takes his time with everything, especially when she isn't here. I hate him. But I'm a guest." I couldn't tell her what he'd done to my mother, but I wouldn't forget it. I didn't know how Mom could just put it aside—how Mom could stand him. More than anything, she seemed to forget how I felt about him staying here. I would be on my guard. But I told myself I would be home with my family of choice soon.

"Does your mother seem happy?"

I exhaled. The room was too warm, and I was sweating. In Florida, I spent a lot of time being too warm. People who live here didn't seem to notice the heat. The phone stuck to my ear. To her question about my mother, I said, "What is happiness?"

"Well, that's a gloomy attitude. What's wrong?"

I knew if my voice rose with anger, it would alarm Grandma, but I felt too tired to pretend. "Mom's doing as she pleases. I just don't want to watch her destroy her life." Then I had a thought from nowhere, and I asked, "Have you heard from Legs?"

Grandma's voice turned hard. It sounded hundreds of miles away, which it was. "You broke up with her. Why should she be in touch with us? You were the attraction to this phone number."

"You talked to her about the new girl. So she has been talking to you."

"True. I shouldn't be trying to help either of you."

"Being here made me realize how much I care for her." Actually, I couldn't imagine my life without her. And I may have screwed my chances up with her by having sex with Lyric. Still, she had told me she was going to see someone else. I thought I could forgive that if she wanted me to. I was going to call her. I just had to decide what to say. I wanted to say I was sorry—that I wanted to work things out. I could text her. But how did I get all of that into a text?

Grandma said, "If you know how much you cared for her, then maybe you're learning."

"I'm flawed," I said. "But now that I've learned that, I'm going to try to fix it. I'm going to try to start up again with Legs."

"I hope that works out for you." She sounded doubtful. But I wasn't going to let that stop me.

Neither of us said anything for a moment. Then Grandma said, "Joyce says hello."

"Tell her hello. Is she done with Virginia Woolf?"

"Her wrist is better—less pain, I mean. She's up and around. Can't say where she's at with Virginia Woolf."

I thought I heard Charlie stirring around in the living room. "I have to go."

Grandma said, "Just let us know your flight number so we'll be there waiting for you."

We exchanged I love yous and hung up.

I stuffed my phone in my back pocket and picked up the black ball cap. I turned it over in my hands and ran my fingers over the white stitching that declared *Seminoles for Sobriety*. The hat had lost some of its shape, but I would always treasure it. I put it in my back pocket and sat there a minute.

As usual, my room was too hot. I got up and headed to the bathroom. I'd slept in my shorts, and when I passed the mirror, I noticed a pooch in my belly. I wondered how much weight I'd gained. These days, I checked my reflection every time I passed that mirror.

Back in my room, I started gathering my clothes to pack. I heard a soft tap at my bedroom door. No one was in the house but me and Charlie. I stayed quiet, pulling on my clothes. He called out my name. Scared and wanting to discourage a conversation, I said, "I'm sleeping."

He twisted the doorknob and pulled it open. My heart pounded. I knew what this guy was capable of.

Charlie slurred his words a little. "Goin' after some beer and smokes. You want anything? I could run through McDonald's. Just say the word."

I picked a sports bra off the floor. "I don't need anything."

He blocked the door. The smile on his face made my skin crawl.

I was trapped, so I walked toward him, thinking he'd step aside.

He stayed in my way, watching me.

"Excuse me," I said. "I need to get out of here."

"What?"

"Get the fuck out of my way."

I couldn't turn my head. He smelled of stale beer and cigarettes. I wasn't sure what else.

He took a step into the room.

My voice was loud. "Get away from me!"

"You are a very pretty little girl." The beer on his breath penetrated the air.

A knot grew in my gut. I was scared, but I wouldn't let him see it. I stepped backward, ready to throw something at him and try to escape.

Then he stopped.

I heard Mom's keys hit the counter. She was home, and this dance was over.

Charlie put his first finger to his lips. Then he disappeared.

I backed up and collapsed on the bed.

A few minutes later, Mom was at my door saying, "I hope you don't have plans tonight. I've picked up groceries and I'm going to cook us dinner."

"Will Charlie be here?"

"No. He left when I came in. I understand your feelings about him. It'll just be the two of us. I want to talk to you over a bowl of chili." She cocked her head. "He hasn't bothered you, has he?"

I shook my head. Why stir things up? I was

leaving anyway. "Just being around him bothers me, especially since he beat you. Please don't leave me alone with him again."

She nodded. Then we stared at each other for a few seconds, and I asked, "Did you get my flight changed?"

"Over the phone. Get the ticket at the check-in desk. I'll get started on dinner as soon as I change my clothes."

"I need to go across the street and to see Mrs. Boyle one last time."

The disappointment showed on her face. "I guess dinner can wait a while."

I felt the urge to embrace her, and then I did. With the exception of the day of the Disney trip, I think it was one of the few times in my life that I ever voluntarily touched her. My eyes teared up a little. "I just had it in my head to do it this way. It isn't much. Mrs. Boyle will be okay if she knows this is a mother-daughter thing."

"I'll start dinner now then. I have so much I want to say to you. I think I'm finally ready."

❧❧❧❧

The landscape in front of Mrs. Boyle's house looked pleasant and new. Flowers sent by the queens and servers at Magnolia's were in clusters with spaces of mulch between them. A flowerbox contained lots of green with small white flowers that poured out like a waterfall. Quite a bit of the yard near the house was marked off with landscape stones. Bunches of flowers were staggered along the edge, and greener plants were in the back nearer to the house. Her grass was freshly cut. The people from Magnolia's were taking care of her. Hers was the only house on the block that, since the hurricane, was in order. Better than it was before.

When she opened the door, she had a friendly smile on her face. "Come in. Come in."

Lyric stood behind her with a paper plate heavy with a sandwich and chips.

"Want a sandwich?" Mrs. Boyle asked. "I've got plenty of ham. Dana's friends at the tattoo shop and Magnolia's bring more food every day."

I shook my head. "I'm eating with my mother pretty soon."

"I won't push you, but there's plenty of chocolate cake in the kitchen."

Lyric said, "I'll get all of us a piece." And he went into the kitchen.

I followed him, saying, "Just wrap my cake up, and I'll take it with me. I shouldn't eat more now."

"No problem." He wrapped a big slice on a paper plate with Saran wrap. He smiled and passed it to me. I reached for it, set it on the counter, and put my arms around him. He pulled me as close as possible. I melted into his embrace, and we kissed. After a moment, still in his arms, I asked myself what the hell I was doing.

I heard Mrs. Boyle behind us. She said, "Oh, excuse me," then backed out of the kitchen.

Our arms dropped, and without a word, we got the cake and made our way into the dining room, following her.

The three of us sat at the table. We passed around a pitcher of sweet iced tea. I noticed something was decidedly different. The usual clutter from the table was gone. In fact, most of the house was straightened up and cleaner than I'd ever seen it.

Mrs. Boyle noticed me looking around. "Once all this attention goes away, I won't know where to find anything. There was a system to my disorder."

"It looks very nice," I said.

They quietly ate a half of a ham sandwich while I sipped my tea, then Lyric said, "I hope you can come down to Magnolia's tonight."

I sighed. In addition to my plans, it looked like everybody else had other ideas for my last night in Florida. I had intended to finish packing and go to bed early. The plane ride would be grueling enough, and just the thought of it alone made me tired. The last few days had been stressful. I loved Lyric, and he loved me. I wanted to please him and started thinking about a way I could go to Magnolia's.

Mrs. Boyle had been so kind, except for the first day when she pulled a rifle on me. She only mentioned my sunburned nose once and made a practice not to stare at it. She seemed to understand the way the atmosphere was at my mother's house, as well as how much time I spent alone. She, with Lyric, helped me get Mom's car out of the ditch after it had been driven home by a woman who had no memory of the trip. Then she dealt with the hurricane at her house and at my mother's. She lost her son but still found it in her heart to help me. If I stayed with her for five years, I could never make up for the kindness she'd shown me. Her life sure hadn't been simple with Dana's murder, and no matter how much his friends worked, they'd never make up for her loss.

I said, "I have an early plane in the morning. I have packing to do, and my mother is cooking dinner. I'm sorry, but I'm booked."

I reached for my tea.

Lyric put his hand over mine. "All your friends want to see you, to say goodbye."

I stammered, "I'll do my best."

Lyric shoved an icing-loaded piece of cake in his mouth and chewed and didn't quite wait until he was finished to say, "I'll help you however I can."

"Okay. I'll get there after dinner. You can help me pack afterward." But as I spoke, doubts rose in my mind.

Chapter Twenty-one
(The Alley)

I didn't feel I'd been in Florida long enough to make many friends, but if the past several weeks were long enough to fall in love, I had to accept that they were long enough to make some friends. The people at Magnolia's and I had been through some tough things together. A hurricane will cement friendships. Bobbie had lost her day job when the merry-go-round had been torn from its anchoring and tossed like a toy into the sea. She'd found a job waiting tables somewhere that she hated. I'd sat and listened to her but could do nothing but that. Others had to rearrange their lives. Things would never be the same.

When Lyric asked me to make one last trip to Magnolia's, I felt a mixture of warmth and anxiety. My time was short.

But he'd insisted, "You're leaving in the morning. It's got to be today." Then he added, "To be honest, they've gone together and got you a little something. It's a going-away surprise party with decorations and balloons. Lady Ann made you a cake. Those people at Magnolia's have taken you in like a sister. You have to give them a chance to say goodbye."

I sighed and said, "I'll try."

The friendship between Lyric and me was confusing. I didn't want to deal with it, but I had to. I'd planned on going back to Illinois and finding Legs, of pleading with her to give us another chance. Now I'd taken a step toward Lyric. I wanted him, but I hadn't meant for us to go so far. When he first touched me, he said for the hundredth time he knew that we were temporary. But sometimes people commit to stuff they just can't manage. Without even knowing it, they cross one boundary after the next. I was determined to go home. We were both clear on that. I was not staying in Florida. He couldn't change my mind. I needed a long talk with Grandma. But that would have to wait. For now, I tried to stick to our agreement, even if some feelings were edging their way to the surface of my heart. I'd learned that I wasn't the type of girl who could make love and then walk away. This was going to hurt.

"Okay, I'll go to Magnolia's," I said. "I can't stay late, though. Will that please you?"

His smile was a little crooked. "That will be perfect." Then he gave me my wrapped-up piece of chocolate cake and a quick hug. "I'm going to miss you."

He planted a second wet kiss on my ear and backed away. "I'm going to the bar ahead of you. When you come, go by the road. A straight couple had a scare two nights ago. You stay out of that alley."

I gave him a mock salute. "Yes, sir."

I left my Slipknot T-shirt lying on top of a suitcase and went into the kitchen. Mom was at the stove. We weren't great talkers, but I made an effort. This was my last day in Florida. I wanted to leave Mom with one good memory.

I asked, "What are you cooking?"

She jumped, startled, and turned to me. "Hi, sweetie, you about ready to eat?"

"Yes. I suppose so."

"I'm cooking chili for your last meal. You used to love my chili."

"I did. Thank you."

Mom said, "The least I could do. I'm afraid you haven't had a very nice visit."

"I'm easy to please." I pulled out a chair and sat at the breakfast table. The sky was still light. I wondered if I had time to eat, go to Magnolia's, and not be too late coming home.

"I've always liked that about you."

When had she noticed that? And if she had, was it true? Regardless, it made me feel happy that she always liked something about me.

She moved toward the island, picked up something, and turned toward me with small salads. "I hope you're hungry."

She set one in front of me with a new bottle of Thousand Island dressing. I could see the remaining pale bruises on her arm and a much faded green and purple place on her cheek, thanks to Charlie, who'd been easily forgiven.

I gathered my courage. "Truth is, I'm going somewhere pretty soon."

"What? You have a six thirty flight tomorrow morning. Do you have time to go anywhere?"

"I'll go after we eat."

"Well, this is your last night in Florida. You're a big girl. I'm sure it'll work out all right."

Thus, we started on our salads. I hadn't eaten since the last of the pizza from the night before. It had been hard to turn down the food across the street to be hungry enough for this meal. Mom even remembered I liked chili. All those years we lived alone together, I didn't think she remembered one day of it, and here she remembered chili.

Later, as we put our dishes in the dishwasher, my mother said, "There's something I want you to know." She didn't wait for me to answer. "It's about your half brother."

My mind was racing. What brother? I'd been an only child all my life. Then I remembered my mother's hint about being pregnant when she left us.

She said, "I left you and your father because I was pregnant. I was sure the guy, the baby's father, would marry me. As you can probably see, I'm not the best judge of men. In any case, you have a half brother who lives with your Aunt Gussy, my youngest sister, in St. Louis. She couldn't have children of her own after a bout with ovarian cancer and surgery. I asked her if she wanted this baby since I was ready to give him up to the Catholic church. Gussy knew a secretary to a lawyer who convinced the lawyer to help us with a legal adoption. I had to say that I didn't know who his father was. Seemed like it took forever, but it finally came through. No one knows the little boy isn't Gussy's, including her second, most current husband or the boy."

Before I could interrupt, she went on.

"You have a right to look him up and meet him. But there are ways it could go wrong, and people you didn't mean to hurt could get hurt. So think about it. Sometimes it's best to let sleeping dogs lie." Grandma's saying. Had she heard it from her, or did all old people say it?

I asked, "Why didn't you ask Dad if you could stay? Or at least come back when the guy abandoned you?"

"I didn't want to hurt you or your father again."

"Maybe I knew my father better than you."

"Stop it, Jeannie. You're giving me chills." She folded her arms across her chest.

I sighed. It was too late for any of that stuff. "I'm sorry."

A moment of quiet was followed by, "You're a lot like your father."

"Thank you."

Next she said, "I did go back once. I was visiting my sister Gabby and her son. They live close to Illinois, so I thought I'd take a day and go up to the old house. I wasn't even sure that you and your dad still lived there. I came to the house and looked in. Everything was in order. It was about time for school to end, so I sat in my car waiting for you. When you came, you were with two other girls, laughing and carrying on. You were much taller, thinner, and healthy looking. When you went into the house with your friends, I backed away and left."

Her lips curled slightly in an unexpected smile. "About this summer, thank you for giving me a chance to get to know you. I hoped you'd stay longer, but with all that's happened, I can't blame you for going back to Grandma's. I understand."

I started to say something again, I don't remember what, but she went on. "I'm proud to have you as my daughter. You're going to have a good life, honey, much better than mine."

At this point, I was speechless.

She was breathing hard. She held up a single finger and went on. "I made a good choice with your father. He and your grandmother have taught you the basics of living a good life. I'm not sure what they are, but you have them."

I threw my arms around her neck and said, "I hope you're right." At that moment, I felt I was pretty screwed up.

I thought I might cry, but she beat me to it. At last, pulling away, she said, "A bit of advice from someone who's been there. Whatever you do as a grownup, no matter how bad things are, don't abandon your children. I've been meaning to tell you since you came here, it's one of my biggest regrets."

Beneath her T-shirt, she felt a little sweaty. I asked myself, was it the temperature of the kitchen or the stress of the conversation?

Dropping her hands, she seemed a little embarrassed by the show of affection. "It's late," she said, "you should go see your friends. You have an early plane in the morning."

My phone rang. I said to Lyric, "I'm on my way."

I thanked Mom for dinner and turned to go.

I'd get to the bar later than I planned. I shoved my phone in my back pocket, pulled Lyric's ball cap down over my head, and left.

❦❦❦❦

I wouldn't have taken the alley, especially after dark, if I hadn't been so late.

Alone, the alley seemed more sinister than ever. I could hear music from the boardwalk. Some spots along the way were lighted; I stuck with them. I found a few dark muddy shadows and avoided them the best I could. Then I caught movement ahead. My heart jumped. Anxiously, I said, "Hello, who's there?"

She was closer than I'd imagined. Without warning, Bobbie was standing before me. I'd met her the first night I'd come to Magnolia's. Then we'd talked as she waited for her day job at the merry-go-round to start several times. She was my friend, a disco drag queen with expensive wigs who lip-synched to Judy Garland. The wig she was currently wearing was askew, but I felt relieved to see her rather than a serial killer.

I said, "Hi. You come out for a cigarette?" Then I realized I hadn't smelled any cigarette smoke.

She smiled nervously. "I came out to meet a guy who hasn't shown up yet."

The condition of her wig told me otherwise. I nodded and started to walk around her.

She reached for my arm and jerked it up behind me. I should have been terrified, perhaps kicked her in the nuts, but I wasn't scared yet. I knew this queen. She was a friend of mine. I'd watched her sing and dance a hundred times.

"Ouch, you're hurting me."

She said nothing but started pulling me toward the opposite side of the alley. To make it easier on myself, I tried to stay in step with her. She pulled me behind a large dumpster and shoved me toward a wall. Both my hands were free at that point, I held them out to stop myself as I slammed into the bricks and slid to the ground. Something softened my fall. It was a moment before I realized I'd landed on top of someone. I rolled over to face Bobbie. She seemed confused. I tried to take advantage of it.

"What in the hell is going on?" I demanded.

"I don't know," Bobbie said. "We were just doing it, and then he passed out."

"We should call an ambulance," I said, even though I was sure it was too late for medical help. And soon, it would be too late for me.

Bobbie's smile was crooked, her eyes insane. "We're friends, right? You won't tell nobody, will you?"

"Of course not. It was just an accident, right?" I wanted to stay friends with her for now. I had to.

"Right." Then she came toward me. I asked myself if it were possible that Bobbie was the person who'd killed at least three men in the past few months, plus scared the hell out of a straight couple a few days ago. It looked bad for Bobbie, being in the alley with a dead body, holding me against my will. I could barely breathe.

I saw it in her eyes. She'd come up with a plan. "I'm going to tie you up until I figure out what to do with you." From behind one of the dumpsters, she pulled a length of rope and came toward me.

I fake sobbed. "Please don't. I haven't done anything to you."

"You'll tell."

"I won't. I promise I won't. I'm leaving the state tomorrow."

If anything, her eyes got stranger. "Stand up and turn around."

My arm hurt. I thought Bobbie might have broken it when she dragged me back here and tossed me against the wall. I could still move my fingers, though. I used my good hand to brace myself and stand. I turned my back toward her.

She took hold of my wrists, forced them behind me, and wrapped a plastic clothesline rope around them several times. She moved closer to the dumpster and tied the end of the rope around a large filthy metal screw. I was forced to stand with my back to it, a dead body between my feet, and face the lady who would probably kill me.

"You don't have to do this," I pleaded. "Please don't hurt me."

I moved my feet to keep my balance and not fall while hanging from the screw. The body on the ground rolled slightly, and I saw it was the first person I'd talked to in Florida, the man who'd offered me his seat. Joe Smith. I sucked in my breath. He was one of the guys I'd suspected of the murders. A straight guy in a gay bar tricking.

I heard a buzzing and realized it was my cellphone.

Bobbie said, "Where is it?" She groped for it without consideration for my pain.

"Back pocket."

She spun me around and dug the thing out. My T-shirt, the Slipknot bride, was covered with dirt, grease, and foul-smelling trash from the dumpster.

"It's your boyfriend," she said, referring to the caller. "He'll probably come looking for you." Bobbie tossed the phone several yards behind her. Her mistake was accidentally answering it.

I said, "I wasn't supposed to see him tonight. He won't look for me. I leave Florida for good soon. You don't have to hurt me. I'll be gone." I was thinking about my own death and saying anything I could think of.

"I'm not going to hurt you. I'm going to kill you and leave. It'll be a couple of days before you're found. Why would anyone suspect me?"

She was right. She had operated a merry-go-round, for Christ's sake! Who would suspect her? Tears rolled down my cheeks.

Then I heard Lyric's voice. Bobbie had answered

the phone, which was always on speaker, before she threw it. I screamed, and he called my name. I screamed again. Bobbie turned and went toward it—maybe to silence it, and I screamed, as long and as loud as I could. I heard Lyric's voice calling me from somewhere in the alley. I opened my mouth and called his name and screamed. Bobbie ran toward me, used her fist on my guts, and backhanded me across the face. My head crashed into the brick wall behind me, leaving me in cold silence.

☙ ☙ ❧ ❧

I opened my eyes to flashing red lights. I could see people's feet and hear voices but not words. Lyric bent over me, saying my name again and again. I had been lifted onto a gurney and was covered by a thin blanket.

"She's awake," Lyric called out. Everyone seemed interested in that.

I rolled my head to the side and vomited my dinner. Much of it went into my hair.

"Oh, shit." Not sure who said it, but the sentiment was clear.

I felt sleepy and closed my eyes again. Two guys lifted me into an ambulance. I woke up in pain and tried to say something.

Lyric, who was next to me, asked, "What?" He leaned close to my clean ear. "The medic gave you fentanyl. Relax and rest."

In the emergency ward, blocked off by white curtains, my mother stood next to my bed, telling me, "They're going to admit you."

I said, "I don't want to stay. I'm going home

tomorrow."

A nurse at my side, adjusting my IV, said, "You'll have to delay your trip. We need to keep you here, at least overnight."

Somewhere, a baby cried. A man and a woman argued in Spanish.

My eyes welled up with tears. The nurse refused to consider my distress and left. Someone passed me a tissue. I dried my cheeks and blew my nose and vomited again.

My mother called the nurse back. I lay there in a mess until two young women cleaned me without complaint, changing me from my first hospital gown to my second. I asked about the clothes I came in with, but got no answer.

I hadn't realized Lyric was still there until he asked, "Have you noticed they're giving you oxygen? You have an IV antibiotic and had something for the pain, which you cried for until they conceded."

I turned my head, trying to find him. He was at the end of my bed next to Mom. A young man came into the small room carrying a laptop and pulled up my chart. "We have a room for you, and they'll be taking you up there soon."

"Why? I'm fine. I want to go home."

The doctor sighed. "We want to make sure you don't have problems with your liver or spleen. You took some hard blows."

I settled back on my pillow, scared.

He went on, "X-ray showed six broken ribs. You appear to have a bad sprain to your right wrist, pain, but no break, and a head injury. Hell of a knot up there, but a CT scan showed no brain bleed."

I didn't remember a painkiller or X-ray. "When

will I go home?"

"We have to do some more tests. But mostly, we have to wait and see."

I said in what I hoped was a snarl, "What type of medicine is wait and see?" But he was gone.

By the time I was in my own room, the scene outside my window, deep purple clouds, announced the coming sunrise. In the presence of that beauty, all I could think was that my flight home would be leaving the airport soon without me.

Before breakfast, a woman brought me a warm blanket and hung another IV bag. I asked Lyric to close the blinds, and with the help of a painkiller, I went back to sleep.

I woke in a panic. I'd dreamed of Bobbie. She'd come into my room. I'd been alone and couldn't find the buzzer for the nurse. I groaned, and Lyric came close.

"What is it?" he asked.

"Where's Bobbie? Did she get away? Will she come here?"

He took my hand. "You're safe. She ran when she heard us coming. The cops found her in her apartment, packing to leave."

It took me a few minutes to form the next question. "Don't you think she could have gotten away if she hadn't gone back to get her things?"

"Probably so. I guess she figured she had a lot of stuff she didn't want to leave. She had two or three wigs worth more than three thousand dollars each."

I was sleepy again. I told Lyric, "A three thousand-dollar wig or a death sentence. That would be an easy choice for me." I rolled onto my side and felt so much pain that I gasped. With Lyric's help, I found a comfortable position, then I was asleep. In a dream, I told myself that Bobbie had been my friend.

❧ ❧ ❧ ❧

I could hear the phone ringing, then Lyric answered it and passed it to me.

Since this whole thing happened, I wanted my grandma. Now I had her and couldn't think what to say. I groaned.

"Honey, is that you?"

I nodded. Lyric took the phone from me and said, "She's a little groggy right now. Her mother has gone home to get some rest. She was here all night. Jeannie is going to be all right." I could only hear his side of the conversation, and I was glad I'd told her about the boy next door.

I reached for the phone when he said, "I don't think you need to come. She'll be on her way home soon."

Lyric passed me the phone again.

Grandma asked, "Are you all right?"

"I am," I said, then I sort of mumbled, "I'll be there soon."

Lyric took the phone from me and turned his back again.

Then the conversation was over.

I asked, "Is she coming?"

"I think so. She acted like she hadn't decided, but then she said she wanted to."

"I've got to get my hair washed. It stinks too much for company."

"They put some goop on it and brushed it out," Lyric said. "It smells better."

"I can still smell it, please."

Next, I studied a hospital menu and placed an order. Lyric offered to help, but I insisted on doing it myself. If I were ever going home, I had to handle my own affairs. Less than half an hour later, a woman brought in a tray. She tried to raise the bed, but the pain in my side was too much. Lyric fed me some scrambled eggs, oatmeal, and toast. I reached a point when I couldn't eat more. A nurse came in with my meds. She asked if I needed something for the pain.

I said, "Yes."

She handed me a small cup of pills. I was worried that I couldn't get them down, but she gave me a glass with a straw. Finished, I managed to set the glass on the nightstand and saw my black Seminoles ball cap that I had worn into the alley.

I asked Lyric, "Where'd you find it?"

"You must have shoved it into your back pocket. When they put you in a hospital gown, you insisted on keeping it with you. It's kind of roughed up. I can get you another if this one is trashed."

I held out my hand, and Lyric placed the cap there. I held the thing to my chest and slept.

Later in the afternoon, a tech and Lyric helped me out of bed to sit in a large chair. My side hurt, but I was glad to be out of bed, if only for a few minutes. After the tech worked on my hair, we turned the TV on to a baseball game, and Lyric fell asleep before I did. The game was over when he woke me.

"Who won?" I asked.

He shook his head. "Missed it."

☙ ❧ ☙ ❧

The lamp was on, and outside, the sky was dark. I thought I was dreaming when I recognized my best friend, Ruthie. I held my arms out to her, and soon she was lying next to me, both of us in an embrace.

I felt pain and told her, "Be careful."

She settled next to me cautiously.

"Did you come alone?"

She shook her head and moved from my view. Grandma stood at the end of my bed.

I asked for help with my pillows. Ruthie got up and stood on one side and Lyric on the other. They took hold of the sheet beneath me and helped me scoot up in the bed. The alarm went off. A tired-looking tech came into my room. I said, "Sorry, my side was bothering me. They helped me get adjusted."

The woman said, "Call for help," and left.

Grandma came to my bedside. "What in the hell happened?"

I didn't know what to say. Lyric started slowly, "Jeannie and I sometimes went to a club called Magnolia's on the boardwalk."

At a certain point, Grandma needed to sit down.

Lyric went on with the story until he finally said, "That's why Jeannie walked right up to her. She thought they were friends."

Grandma got up out of her chair and came to me. She put her arms around me and pulled me toward her chest. It was soft and smelled a little of fabric softener. "Oh, my God, do you know how close you were to death?"

My grandma wasn't like other grandmas. She was my baby boomer grandma. Her hair had turned into tight curls when it went gray. She wore peasant blouses or T-shirts with sports teams. Never a plain T-shirt or a dress. Her jeans were faded, and some were patched. She carried a large leather purse, so full she could barely lift it or find anything. She couldn't bring her gun on the plane, so it was at home in her glove box. I held my face to her chest and started sobbing into her. I couldn't get much air and eventually turned my head. She let go and returned to the big chair.

Later, a different doctor came in and went over several tests with me. He asked if I still had a headache. I honestly had forgotten about it. "No serious injuries to the spleen or liver. You'll have some pain for a while. Plus, your ribs and wrist will be sore. You'll need a lot of rest."

He asked if I thought I could eat dinner. In fact, I felt hungry. He picked up the hospital menu and handed it to me.

I asked about going home.

He said he didn't know.

I think that was what they were supposed to say. Don't get anyone's hopes up.

He shook hands with Ruthie, Grandma, and Lyric, took one last look at his notebook, and left.

I thought I might be able to go home in the morning, provided I was stable. I wanted to get on a plane right then, but even if I were released that evening, there wasn't another flight until the morning.

Everyone had left to look for a good restaurant, which was difficult since the storm. The restaurant where Mom worked sounded good to everyone. Even my grandma seemed to like the idea. I was alone for a few hours. By then, I'd made a plan for the next couple of days. If I was released sometime tomorrow, Grandma, Ruthie, and I would stay at my mother's house overnight. I pictured us playing cards or talking about everyone on the basketball team, anything but Florida. I missed Grandma and Ruthie so much; it would be several days before I let either of them sleep. We'd take the plane the next day, and I'd be home in Illinois. The last several days, it seemed that no matter how much I wanted to go home, something or somebody was in the way. I felt like a mule trying to get a carrot dangling in front of it. The carrot was home.

≈≋≈≋

At dusk, long shadows fell across the room. A TV game show droned on. The door to the hallway swung open. Startled, I saw someone walk up next to me. I turned my head, and there standing before me was Legs. I swallowed and stammered, "What…how?"

"Your grandma called me. She told me you would be okay, but I wanted to see for myself. How are you?"

"I'm having some pain, but I'll be all right as soon as I get home."

She took a step closer. "I've missed you so much."

"Even while dating this new woman? Have you had her in bed yet?" As soon as the words slipped out, I regretted them. I'd been so determined to do better when I saw her again, and here I'd said the worst thing I could say. I'd wanted to be mature about this. Most of it was my fault. I'd been the one who had choices. Why was I so obnoxious?

Legs staggered backward as if I'd hit her in the gut with an aluminum bat. She took a deep breath. "Fair enough. I did like her. But there could never be anything between her and me. She was in the house to stay sober. Except she couldn't do it. She didn't care much for my brother. But even if it had worked out, I would have missed you and loved you and never been completely hers."

I saw then that Legs had changed. Her hair was longer, and dark roots showed. She was thinner. Only a few months ago, she'd been muscular and solid.

Still angry, I said, "So you came here to see if I could ever forgive you?"

"I was wrong to leave you without trying harder to work things out. I'm sorry." She didn't mention that she needed to forgive me for the ugly things I'd said and done. It took some time for me to figure out that I had been way out of line.

Grandma told me I would regret leaving. She was right. I tried to say what it was all about. "You abandoned me."

"I'm sorry."

I doubted if she understood what being abandoned meant to me. Nevertheless, it was mine to work on. It never had been others who had to change. It had always been me. Why couldn't I just say that?

"I brought you something," she said and held out a paper bag. "I know it won't make it all go away, but it's a start."

I opened the bag and inside I found a pink T-shirt. I knew before I unfolded it that it was a Slipknot tee called Torn Apart. I moaned, then said, "I love it."

A tech came in with my dinner tray and placed it in front of me. Legs stepped back and said, "I should leave and let you eat your dinner."

"Please stay a little longer."

She turned to the tech and asked if it would be all right if she stayed. The tech said, "She's probably going home tomorrow. She's strong enough for company."

Legs pulled up a chair, sat down, and talked

to me while I ate. She told me about the school for paralegals, which she would finish soon and advance. She described the small room that she shared with her brother. He'd had trouble adjusting to the new place at first but was doing better. Legs smiled when she told me that he "made a friend. Something he'd never done before."

I heard a sound from across the room, and Legs said, "Come here and see Jeannie."

I hadn't noticed that Legs's brother had been sleeping in a soft chair across the room. He heard his sister and came around the curtain, and climbed up on my bed. I scooted over to make room for him. He laid his head on my shoulder and put one arm around me. I felt a little pain but managed to stand it. I hadn't realized the kid had been so attached to me. I thought I'd just been part of the wallpaper to him. We shared french fries from my dinner. He soon tired of them.

Legs said, "Now be careful. Jeannie is hurt in her middle."

He loosened his hold but didn't move. Finally, he wiggled down and sat in the closest big chair. Legs found a TV show he liked, and he was soon asleep again.

"He's missed you, asks about you in his own way. The bus trip has wiped him out."

I hesitated, then took a sip of my now cold coffee.

Legs said, "I couldn't stand it if something happened to you. I've loved you for so long..."

"I'm pretty tough." I hadn't felt so tough in that alley with a serial killer. I'd been sure I was going to die.

She took hold of my hand. "Let's figure out how we can get through the next several months."

Legs stayed until visiting time was over. She had a bus to catch and a long ride back to Miami. She kissed me and said she'd text. I wanted more but told myself waiting was part of loving her.

❧❧❧❧

I'd come home from the hospital the next afternoon. While everyone else was exhausted, I felt restless. So I went out to the patio for a few minutes. Lyric came over, and we talked about the way Magnolia's had changed since the hurricane. I went into the kitchen and brought out a couple of Cokes. Lyric ran home and brought a small cake from Magnolia's, the one Lady Ann made. It had wobbly letters around the top—*Bon Voyage, Jeannie*. Plus something in a beautiful gift bag. I reached in and pulled out a black Magnolia's T-shirt.

I put my arms around him and said, "I love it. I will never forget you or Magnolia's."

Lyric stayed with me, and we spent a lazy evening just keeping each other company.

I was half asleep when he said, "Legs visited you last night."

I nodded. Frankly, I wasn't ready to tell him.

"It was good of her to come."

"Yes. We're going to try to work things out."

He looked down for a minute, then said, "You told me from the beginning that was the deal."

"I have feelings about us," I admitted. "But I haven't changed my mind."

"Then I want to say I have a large capacity to love. If there's ever a chance to be more than friends, please say so."

He was quiet then. And I realized we weren't

going to argue. I loved him a little more for that. My family bought a few pizzas for dinner—pizza, I had learned, was the dinner staple of Florida—and Lyric stayed and ate with us. The sun was setting when he left.

Later, the sky was clear, the stars showed magnificently, and the moon was high. Although they were there, I'd gotten to the point that I no longer heard the roar of the insects.

The night reminded me of one summer when my father and I sat on the back porch together. Our air conditioner was broken, and the house was too warm. We'd made big glasses of iced tea and took them to the back porch. It was a Friday night, and Dad asked about homework.

I said, "I'll go to the library tomorrow and do it. It'll be air-conditioned there."

He seemed satisfied. "Good idea."

Right then, I loved him more than anyone in the world.

I'd thought those days with my father would never end. They did.

When my mother told me that, at one time, she'd loved him more than anything, I was sure she must have meant the father I'd known that summer, the man to some degree he'd always been to me. I've sometimes wondered, then and since then, what my dad would have thought about Lyric and my love for him.

Inside the house, my grandma was resting on Mom's couch. Ruthie was sacked out in my room. We would share my twin bed and leave early for the plane.

Driving home from the hospital, I saw more wrath from the hurricane. I wanted everything beautiful again. Debris still dotted the ground; the cleanup was far from finished. More stacks of trash would need to be picked up by intermittent trucks that scanned the neighborhoods. I wondered for how long.

The water from my mother's pool made moving reflections on the side of what was left of the garage. I stretched out on the chaise lounge again. I was sure the chairs didn't belong to us but was puzzled about where to return them. One we'd found a block away and the other more so. I was tired, but my thoughts wouldn't be still. I wanted to get home again, where the weather was normal, just a tornado now and then.

Chapter Twenty-two
(Back Home)

In my nightmares, I asked myself how a woman could be your friend, sing your song, and then try to kill you. How could she sit and give comfort to the mother of her victim? I wondered if I ever knew anything about anyone. I'd looked into Bobbie's eyes and knew I'd been wrong about her—we all had. The dreams went on for what seemed like a long time.

That following winter, I'd sit in my bedroom and look down at the snowy landscape and remember the hot days and nights in Florida. Diablo, from the time I carried my suitcase into Grandma's house, followed me everywhere. He waited at the door when I went to school. He sat with me while I did my homework. He slept with me. I tried to start him on the rug beside the bed, but he pushed himself up to the end of the bed, and when I woke, whenever I woke, he was curled up beside me. Grandma fussed at me about the dog in my room, but I was sure she knew that we curled up together every night to keep the demons away.

I graduated high school midterm and started community college the spring semester. This required extra classes and extra studying. College started with basic studies. I can't say I loved it all, but it was a means to an end. Sometime that winter, between schoolwork and a sixty-five-pound guard dog, the nightmares went away.

It was the pain of losing Diablo that next summer

that finally sent me to counseling for the goddamned abandonment mess.

I texted Lyric often that winter. Once he told me that the boy surfer who'd rented a board from Ron Don's had started to win some winter competitions. I had little to tell him except that to my disappointment, Legs had started a two-year college in Miami for the spring session. I was upset, but I would try to join her, even though I didn't know how I'd afford it. After that, I'd see him on Facebook and always left a comment or at least a thumbs-up. I knew he'd started college that spring, too. Once he mentioned that Betsy came with him.

Then one Saturday morning, I was drinking coffee and fooling around on Facebook, and there it was. Lyric had moved on. In a large picture, he stood next to Betsy in front of a church. Him in a dress suit and her in a poofy white wedding gown. A little boy, hardly more than a toddler, stood close at her side, holding her hand, peeking around the folds of her white skirt.

Lyric had married into a ready-made family. I couldn't think of anything that would make him happier.

The smaller pictures in the same posting showed Betsy with bridesmaids and both of them with their sets of parents. The one I liked the most was of the guys: ushers and the best man. Lyric stood in the center of these guys, a little boy on his hip. The kid's sleepy head resting on his new father's shoulder.

Sometimes I wonder if he ever told Betsy about our trip home from Disney World. I never had the opportunity to tell Legs. I always thought that the betrayal wasn't the sex, but the fact that we declared our love, that we did love each other.

Epilogue
(Ten years later)

I carried my big baking pan filled with a thawing twenty-pound turkey and some kitchen utensils out to the car. Jess followed me, carrying Ava, who started crying before she was strapped in her car seat.

Jess said, "She thinks she's going to the babysitter."

The last time she went there, she stayed the weekend so Jess and I could get away to celebrate our anniversary.

"Be firm," I said, but then I remembered how much I'd hated leaving her overnight.

Jess said, "Do you want to do this?" She strapped Ava into her seat and handed her the musical kitty. When that didn't work, she dug in the diaper bag for a baby cookie. Ava stopped crying.

"Don't you see that she's learning all she has to do is cry to get a cookie?"

"I don't care," Jess said. "I'm getting a headache."

Jess closed the back door and opened the front passenger. She strapped herself in and sat back. I drove through town toward the highway. I'd been gliding along for a while when Jess took my hand and put a soft kiss on it.

I smiled at her. "This trip should be interesting with Ava in her terrible twos."

We were going to Grandma's. I'd been packing the car all morning. We would only stay for the weekend. Jess had to work Monday. I would help Grandma cook a huge Thanksgiving dinner. As Grandma has gotten older, more of that meal fell to me. But I didn't mind the cooking. I hated the salads, so Aunt Sis, my father's sister, brought those. We were trying to get Ava to eat vegetables, but I didn't want them myself, so it was an uphill battle.

We lived in a duplex in Chicago. Our upstairs neighbors, a couple of gay guys, Steve and D.J., were the owners; we leased their downstairs two-bedroom. Our landlords didn't have a problem watching our two cats while we were gone because they had four of their own. They would look in on the two brown striped females we got three years ago when we thought I'd never get pregnant. A month later, the test tube worked.

Last year, my mother came from Florida to Grandma's to spend the weekend. She and Grandma had to get past some difficult moments. But Ava had been a year old, and both grandmas wanted their share of baby-holding and playing.

My mother and I sat up late Friday night, and she told me the story of ending it with Charlie. She'd started back to AA and had a new sponsor, a police officer, who helped her and knew how to put just the right pressure on Charlie, in just the right place. That night we talked, Mom told me she was living alone and liking it.

Ruthie wouldn't come to Thanksgiving dinner—she has her own family—but she would be there for leftovers, pie, and coffee Thursday night. Legs would probably be home for the weekend, visiting her foster mother. Grandma and Joyce no longer lived in her neighborhood, but Legs would come by the new house

Friday or Saturday to visit. At times, even now, I couldn't help imagining what life would be like raising a baby with Legs. Jess was new at a big law firm and worked ungodly hours. Legs would be home. With her foster care background, she would spoil the kid. On Saturdays, Legs and I would lie in bed for the better part of the day.

Every time I saw her, this game of "what if" ran through my brain, and I wondered if her mind was doing the same. A long-distance romance had been impossible for us. When we parted, I was with Jess, and Legs was starting up with someone else.

When Jess went back to work after the baby, and I was left home alone, imagining me with Legs was easier, too easy. We emailed or texted almost daily. I missed her humor and her easy ways. Then, one day I was feeding my nine-month-old Ava, and she reached toward my shoulder. I glanced at her little fingers and saw my treble clef tattoo that I'd gotten that torrid summer all those years ago. I said, "Bird." She blew some bubbles but couldn't quite say it. She had recently acquired the word, "no," and did well with that. I then offered her a bite of pears, but quickly put the spoon in my mouth, and she laughed and laughed.

After that, it all fell away. Before me sat this little person with baby food on her nose and her hair in messy blond curls, a little girl I would never leave. She was high maintenance, of course, but we could play. And that was what I needed, along with a new story to send to my mother.

Check out Martha's other book.

Me Inside - ISBN - 978-1-943353-19-4

Me Inside is a-true-to-life story with a broad appeal. It's a family drama, speckled with just a touch of romance/coming out (but not angst-y) of mystery/intrigue.

It begins when Jeannie Baker's mother abandons her at a very young age, which turns out to be the best thing that ever happened to her. She's left alone with a father who provides a good childhood for her, with all the things she needs, from blue jeans that fit, to a hot breakfast, and to the steady and dependable life she's never had. Then when Jeannie is fifteen years old, a high school basketball star, with good friends and a happy future, her father is murdered…